THE UNTOLD TRUTH OF CLUB
門神
THE MISSION

BY: HEMIE YAO

Special thanks to Tracy Chen

Dedicated to my mother, Tracy Chen, who gave me many amazing ideas for this book series, brainstormed, edited, and fixed the plot with me. It's almost impossible to describe how much she helped me.

The Untold Truth of Club 門神
The Mission
Copyright © 2023 by Hemie Yao.
All Rights Reserved

TABLE OF CONTENTS:

Prologue 7

Chapter 1: Touch of Death 12

Chapter 2: The Mystery Begins 14

Chapter 3: The Art of War 20

Chapter 4: The Big Reveal 29

Chapter 5: Two Principals: Past and Present 38

Chapter 6: The After-School Club 46

Chapter 7: One Chance 58

Chapter 8: Wisdom Has it All 69

Chapter 9: Showdown at The Mahjong Tournament 80

Chapter 10: Paiya Temple 100

Chapter 11: A Figure in The Rain 113

Chapter 12: Disease Disaster 118

Chapter 13: The Rogue Wave 126

Chapter 14: An Unexpected Friend 145

Chapter 15: Bo's Redemption 158

Chapter 16: Truth Monster 170

Chapter 18: The Missing Dragon 179

Chapter 17: The Weathered Notebook 191

Chapter 18: Mysteries Deepen 205

Acknowledgements 210

About the Author 211

PROLOGUE

Floods surrounded the Earth. Countless homes were destroyed, farmland disappeared, and numerous lives were lost. Gonggong, the water god, isn't the only god capable of creating floods, but he was recklessly abusing his power more than any other god or goddess. To make matters worse, there was an infamous duel to claim the throne of heaven between Gonggong and Zhurong, the god of fire. After Gonggong lost the fight, he angrily made a tear in the sky out of pure frustration. Some legends say he was killed, others say he was banished to an undisclosed place.

— THE BET

What actually happened was that the Jade Emperor, the ruler of all heavens, got increasingly fed up with Gonggong's madness. Before the duel took place, the Jade Emperor devised a plan.

To set his plan in motion, the Jade Emperor paid a visit to a dragon, who was once a boy known for swallowing a fiery pearl and becoming a dragon as a result. The Jade Emperor convinced the dragon to lend him its pearl for one time only. This pearl is capable of fulfilling one's wish if it's placed in the right setting. The dragon agreed and spat out the pearl, transforming back into the boy it once was.

The Jade Emperor put the pearl in his gold oval jar designated for jades. Twenty-four hours later, a blue-greenish Jade shaped like a water drop appeared inside the jar. The pearl was returned to the boy as promised.

Next, the Jade Emperor summoned Gonggong, the water god, to his palace.

"Gonggong, it came to my attention that you and Zhurong have scheduled a fight," The Jade Emperor voiced calmly. "I'm offering you a bet. If you win the duel, I'll leave you alone for ten thousand years. If you lose, I'll activate a jade to take over your control of water."

A servant brought out a silver tray holding the oval jar. Inside was the shining Jade.

Gonggong let out a laugh. "A tiny jade to take my power?"

The Jade Emperor spoke again, "All you have to do is to bless this Jade with your power before the duel takes place. If you win, I'll destroy it immediately."

Gonggong squinted his eyes for a minute. "Ten thousand years is worth it," he said arrogantly. "I accept."

As legend says, Gonggong lost the duel. He was furious, but the bet was in effect. The Jade Emperor activated the Jade.

二. THE TEMPLE

The Jade still wouldn't work yet, not until it was placed in a temple on the Earth to fully enable its power. Shortly after the duel, the Jade Emperor ordered Lu Ban, god of craftsmanship, to erect a temple in a rural area of northern China to keep the Jade. Once the Jade was in the correct location inside the temple, it would take control of Gonggong's power and stop him from producing devastating floods.

Some time ago, Lu Ban got into an argument with the Jade Emperor over architecture. Lu Ban didn't want to do any favors for the emperor as he was still salty about it, but he couldn't disobey either. Instead, he saw this as an opportunity for revenge.

As ordered, Lu Ban made a secure space inside the temple surrounded by many boobytraps to keep the Jade protected. However, he discreetly structured a hidden tube which led to an easy way out, hoping one day somebody would take the Jade away and anger the Jade Emperor. It wasn't much, but Lu Ban's options for revenge were limited.

In the meantime, the Jade Emperor created a Fenghuang, a beautiful and tall bird to live at the temple and guard the Jade at all times. Seemingly odd-looking, Fenghung had body parts of many different animals and a long tail in five sacred colors, red, yellow, green, black, and white. It emitted a soft golden glow that followed everywhere it went.

While Lu Ban was building, Fenghuang held the Jade in its beak watching but didn't notice the hidden tube as it was well camouflaged with the surroundings. Once completed, Fenghuang swooped down, maneuvered gracefully through the boobytraps, and placed the Jade precisely in the designated spot.

The Jade instantly gained control over Gonggong. Although he remained free, Gonggong lost the ability to cause floods. The Jade Emperor was pleased.

二. THE PEASANT

Occasionally, an old peasant who lived on a farm near the temple came to clean the place out of respect. Fenghuang knew the peasant was a harmless human being, so it never bothered him.

On a sunny morning without a single cloud in the sky, the peasant came to the temple again. While cleaning, the peasant unknowingly pressed a little piece of decorative wood on the wall. Suddenly, distant noises filled the air, sounding like a rock rushing down a slim stone tube. The sound finally stopped.

In front of him, a little box popped out of the wall with red fabric inside, holding a blue-greenish, water-drop-shaped Jade. The peasant picked it up and held it to the light. The Jade gave a pattern of dark blue specks that reminded him of the nightly sky.

The old man had grown up in a poor family and never saw anything like this. The gem dazzled him enough to make a spur-of-the-moment decision. He decided to bring the Jade home, thinking it wasn't a big deal because he never saw anyone else come to this temple. The peasant gingerly placed the Jade in his palm and pushed the empty box back. Walking home with the Jade in his pocket, the old man didn't realize his action would cause the deaths of many lives.

Upon returning home, the peasant's family was amazed by the precious stone. They cherished it very much as they would pass it down through each generation within the family.

At the time when the Jade was removed from the temple, Fenghuang was perched on top of the temple in perfect view of everything, but it had fallen asleep under the warm sun, not worrying about the peasant.

When Fenghuang finally woke up from its cozy nap, it realized in horror that the Jade was gone. Fenghuang was punished by the Jade Emperor who turned it into wood for thousands of years to come.

Floods started again.

CHAPTER 1:
TOUCH OF DEATH
February 3 (Sunday 10pm)

MODERN-DAY, CHINA

I thought nothing else would happen for the rest of the night, but I was wrong.

I barely fell asleep when I heard a loud thud downstairs. Minutes later, running footsteps were pounding on the floor below me, with an eruption of worried voices.

"What happened?"

"Is she okay?"

I jumped out of my bed. Obviously, I wasn't the only one who heard it. A few students rushed downstairs along with me.

A crowd of students already stood there in a circle. In the center were a few school medics on their knees attending someone on the floor. One of them signaled the crowd to quiet down.

It's Pingye! She appeared to be motionless and...lifeless. *What happened to her? She was fine just hours ago!* A lump formed in my throat. Everyone watched on while the medics transferred Pingye to a stretcher and carried her away.

I spotted Lingling in the crowd. "Lingling, what happened?" I was almost afraid of hearing the answer.

Lingling turned around with the look of a full-on panic attack. Her breath was short and quick. I had never seen her like that. Tears kept running down Lingling's face, which she didn't even bother to wipe away. Lingling glanced at me and sped away.

"Lingling?" I was frightened, not just for Pingye but for Lingling as well.

"Not now." Lingling continued walking, her voice shaking.

The crowd of students had slowly dispersed one by one. By this time, only one other person was still here. It was Lu.

Lu slumped against the wall, stone-faced with wet eyes. He stared at the floor blankly, like a completely different person from who he was yesterday.

"Lu, are you okay? What happened to Pingye?"

"I don't know." Lu sounded deeply distressed, avoiding eye contact with me. Which question he was answering, I wasn't sure.

The air was heavy. The night was dreadful. Lu eventually got up and departed without another word.

BEEP, BEEP, BEEP. A loud siren suddenly went off, breaking the deadly silence. *What now?*

"Everyone, please stay inside," A loudspeaker repeated. "This is a flash flood warning."

CHAPTER 2:
THE MYSTERY BEGINS
November 13 (Tuesday)

TWO AND HALF MONTHS AGO

I have no idea why I'm here. Shortly after I turned thirteen, I was sent to a boarding school deep in the woods without a reason.

It has been a week since I arrived. The school seemed normal at first, but unexplainable things started happening around me. For instance, I've heard students sharing odd stories. Well, you bet I want to get to the bottom of it! One day at a lunch table in the cafeteria, I finally got the nerve to question it.

"Listen! You won't believe what happened to me yesterday!" One student exclaimed with wide eyes.

"What happened?" Everyone turned their heads to him.

"I almost forgot to open my eyes!"

In a heartbeat, long gasps came from everyone sitting at the table, except...me. Feeling confused, I asked, "What's wrong with that? Don't we close our eyes when we sleep?"

This time, everyone at the table immediately turned to stare at me with shocked eyes, except a lone person laughing

THE UNTOLD TRUTH OF CLUB 門神

until he realized I was serious. It was like a bee suddenly realized the flower was plastic.

What did I say wrong? Forgot to open his eyes? What does that even mean?

They looked at each other in silence and suddenly became fascinated by the food on their trays.

What happened next? That's the thing because I don't know! This was the last memory I had before I found myself standing in my dorm room alone. I tried long and hard to recall what had happened after the conversation at the cafeteria, but my memory was plain blank. It was a freaky feeling forgetting something that happened so recently. Do you ever have those moments when you forget what you ate for dinner last night? Well, I can tell you it wasn't like that.

Am I losing my mind?

In addition, the fact that this school is only four hours long with an after-school club that lasts three hours is something. I'm not complaining, but I doubt any after-school club needs to be almost as long as the school day, right? Not to mention every student seems to be in the same club, the one-and-only club! I thought it must be mandatory so I asked the assistant principal, Ms. Wu, if I could join.

"No, I'm afraid not." She brushed it off without giving a reason.

You may ask why I write in English while living in China. Well, my name is Cassidy Giordano. Right off the bat, I'm pretty sure you can tell I'm not a native Chinese. I'm Caucasian. I was born in Milan, Italy, where my family spoke English most of the time. When I was five, my parents took me on our last trip to China where they died unexpectedly.

Ever since, I had been living in an orphanage in Beijing until last week.

I was lucky enough to learn both Chinese and English since the orphanage is bilingual. As far as why I write in English, it's a lot easier in my opinion. For instance, this is how you write red in Chinese - 紅色的, and this is how you write zero in Chinese - 零. I personally think it's much faster to write in English.

Anyway, I arrived at my new school a week earlier than I was supposed to, *so I was told*. I've been exploring the area on my own and got lost a few times.

My school sits within a forest on the mountains, at the outskirts of Shen Zheng. It's huge, with the black fence merging into the forest so you can't see it easily. In the center of the front fence lies a magnificent black gate. Inside, there's a large lawn in the middle, two dorm buildings on either side, and a vast plain building in the back. A vegetable garden resides in the far-left corner, with a few bulky water barrels and a well next to it. On the far-right side is an extensive wooded area.

Compared to Beijing, southern China is full of greenery, a lot warmer, less windy, and much easier to breathe without the air pollution. I began to like this area, despite the weirdness at the school.

Finally, I started classes yesterday, which were surprisingly normal. I was supposed to meet with Principal Jiang on my first day, but our meeting was postponed to Friday because he was in the hospital.

Today, I saw the word 打 (fight) on Mei's schedule. Why 打? I guess it's not impossible that I was seeing things, so I asked her. By the way, Mei Cao is my roommate who was assigned to me randomly. She's my closest friend so far.

"Oh, it's a typo for...数学 (*math*)," Mei murmured.

If 打 could be a typo for 数学, they need to check what's wrong with the person who typed it.

It was sundown when I made a quick run to the cafeteria to pick up my jacket that I left earlier. I caught wind of something that I really wish I didn't.

Behind a half wall separating the kitchen and the common area in the cafeteria, there was a group of students cleaning the kitchen. I wasn't going to eavesdrop, but one word made me stop cold.

"...Cassidy."

"I know, right? It makes no sense that they sent her here. She doesn't have a clue about us!"

"Yeah, not to mention she's white!"

One sighed. "No one cares about her race!"

"I've never seen a white person before."

"Well, if you leave the school for once, maybe you'll see someone who looks different from you!"

"Yeah, white people walk on the streets just like us."

"But she's the only white student here, isn't she?"

"Yes, but people are people."

"Not in my book."

Someone sighed.

My vision blurred as my eyes got watery. It was ridiculous. One of the reasons why I even looked forward to this school was hoping that people would be more open-minded.

What should I do? Should I confront them or leave without being seen? What's the secret of this school? It's obvious that they don't want me to find out, but why? There was so much going through my head at once that I decided I should just bail out.

I dragged my feet back to my room with my jacket around my arm. Pushing the door open, I saw Mei sitting at a wooden desk against the wall, inspecting the leaves of a flower taken from the windowsill where her plants flourished. The large white prints of "Reduce Reuse Recycle" stood out on the back of her green hoodie.

I plopped down on the lower half of the bunk bed. I silently stared at the cut-out snowflakes and intricate dragons that hung from the ceiling, as well as the crescent moon dreamcatcher above my head that Mei made for me, identical to hers.

My thoughts were running wild. I hadn't broken my train of thought, replaying the conversation in my head over and over again. *It makes no sense that they send her here because she doesn't have a clue. Obviously, there's something I don't know, but I'm trying to fix that! What don't I know? I don't know what they meant by not opening their eyes. I'm not allowed to join the after-school club, so I can't explain whatever happens there.*

Subconsciously, I was still trying to figure out the secret. *Looks like my brain won't stop until I know.*

"Mei, what do you do in the after-school club?" I turned to Mei.

Mei spun around. Her long braids fell from her shoulder. Her arched eyebrows were partially hidden by her bangs.

"Huh?" Mei was caught off guard. "What? Oh, it's a …" A long pause. "…book club."

"What?" Now *I* was caught off guard. I doubt all the students want to participate in a three-hour book club every day.

"Yeah, it's a thing about flowers…and stuff," Mei said in a sluggish tone while getting up and climbing to her bed above mine. "Well, I had a really long day. I'm going to sleep now." Mei pulled a blanket over her head. Immediately, she began to snore. Her snoring came suspiciously quick and unnaturally loud.

It was a bad lie in a funny way. I tried to make sense of Mei's response, but I shouldn't analyze it too much because she probably made it up.

It did confirm my suspicion that something unusual is happening in the after-school club. A book club about flowers and stuff? Not Likely.

I'll find out more tomorrow. Somehow, the cafeteria incident was already behind me.

CHAPTER 3:
THE ART OF WAR
November 14 (Wednesday)

I spent hours in the afternoon searching about our school on the only computer in the dorm. It was giving me a headache, so I decided to take a break. I strolled in the woods and came upon a small, crystal-clear pond. It was near the corner of the fence. I saw a girl with her hair wrapped in a perfect bun, wearing a blue T-shirt and blue jeans.

Sitting on the edge of the pond, the girl was staring at a white and blue-striped pot full of water. It was the size of two palms and shaped like a squeezed pumpkin. I vaguely heard her mumbling under her breath.

"Hello?" My voice was like a whisper that I could barely hear myself. I wasn't sure which way was ruder, disturbing her or walking away without saying hi.

"What?" The girl suddenly turned her head to me. She had tanned skin and high cheekbones. "You're...Cassidy Giordano?"

I became a little wary, in disbelief that a stranger knew me already. "Yes, I am. How do you know?"

THE UNTOLD TRUTH OF CLUB 門神

"Well, you're all people have been talking about lately." She shrugged.

Slightly embarrassed, I started fiddling with my fingers. Unsure of what to say, I asked for her name.

"Lingling Sun."

"Hi, Lingling. So…what are you doing with the pot?" I asked as if I just noticed it.

"I was washing my face."

"At the pond?"

"My dorm is too crowded because everyone comes to talk," Lingling answered. "My twin brother, Lu, told me all about the 'interesting' rocks he found here." She made air quotes.

Lingling was convincing, but it didn't explain why she was talking to the water…unless she was talking to herself. Nevertheless, I was reluctant to believe her, especially with other people making goofy excuses to me…cough, cough, Mei (yes, I know you can't cough in words).

I tried to come up with a topic for conversation. To my relief, Lingling started nattering after she dumped the water into the pond and put the pot in her backpack.

"Take a look at this rock." Lingling grinned, grabbing one out of the water, with tiny bits of sparkles under the sunlight. "I'll show it to Lu."

"Do you collect rocks too?"

"No, I paint them while Lu collects them. He claims they're interesting, forming millions of years ago waiting to be discovered." Lingling straightened her back, lifted her chin and said proudly, "But *I* make them interesting!"

I smiled. Lingling pocketed the rock and then turned to me. "So, how do you like it here?"

I shrugged, not so sure.

"Well, you'll like it," Lingling said with certainty. "Our New Year's Eve parties are always fun. It's coming up in a little over two months. This year, we're going to start an annual Mahjong tournament."

"What? Mahjong?" I busted with excitement. Mahjong is my favorite game. I played a lot at my last orphanage. "THERE'S A TOURNAMENT?" I shouted so loud that birds flew out of the trees.

Lingling nodded and smiled at me. "You can still sign up. There'll be a pre-qualification round in a few days."

"Of course! Where do I register?" It sounded amazing. A whole event dedicated to Mahjong. I never participated in anything like that.

"Library. I'll go with you."

"Thank you!" With a wide grin, I practically skipped along following Lingling.

"I never played Mahjong. Is it easy to learn?" Lingling asked.

"It's simple." I slowed down. "Four players sit at each side of a table. They build four stacks of cards first. Then one person rolls a dice to determine where to pick the first four cards."

"Why do they do that?" Lingling asked while we walked toward the building.

"To make sure no one cheats while building the deck," I explained. "After that, all players take turns to assemble a total of thirteen cards. Each player draws a new card and discards a least useful card. They keep going around and around until someone wins or cards from the stack are exhausted."

THE UNTOLD TRUTH OF CLUB 門神

"How do you know if you win?"

"You need four sets of three cards and a pair to win. Once you are about to win pending the last card, you need to declare 'I'm calling.'"

"That must take a while."

"Not as long as you think. Lastly, if you get a flower card, you can draw an extra card. Each flower card gives a bonus if you win. That's basically it." I smiled at Lingling, trying to make the game sound as easy as possible.

"Those are a *lot* of rules," Lingling concluded, shaking her head.

We arrived at the library, coming to a stop at a tiny stool with a mailbox-like cube and a basket of papers on top. I took a piece of paper and jotted down my name. Right when I was about to drop it in the box, a voice came out of nowhere.

"Why is she here?" Someone said in dismay.

My hand paused before I turned around. Two boys were right behind me, completely polar opposites. One short and one tall. One dark-skinned and the other light toned.

"I'm signing up," I said.

"Can't you see the problem, *Lingling*?" the short one said, saying her name like it was an insult.

"No, I can't, Guo." Lingling shot back.

"A white skin wants to play Mahjong," The tall one said as if I wasn't there. I was stunned by the insult.

"Your skin's light too, Ming." Lingling pointed out.

"At *least* I'm Chinese." Ming snickered.

"No matter what you say, Cassidy can play if she wants to," Lingling said firmly.

I took it as a cue to put the paper in the box, although half of my excitement was destroyed.

Guo rolled his eyes and said, "No matter what, Cassidy is going to lose."

"Yep, and I'll make sure to say I told you so," Ming said sneeringly. He scribbled his and Guo's names on two pieces of paper and dropped them in the box.

"You should consider withdrawing." Ming walked away with a flourish, followed by Guo one step behind.

Once out of earshot, Lingling said confidently to me, "They're scared of you."

"What?" I said in disbelief, still upset.

"Why else would they ask you to withdraw? Do you remember the idiom 虚张声势?" Lingling asked.

"Of course." The idiom means *false bravado to bluff*.

"They're scared of being proven wrong, so they bluffed to scare you off." Lingling continued with her theory.

I was intrigued.

"We studied the book *The Art of War* by Sun Tzu in history class." Lingling sounded like a war expert. "I think Ming and Guo used a tactic we learned from the book. Master Sun said all warfare is based on deception. If an army is weak, it must appear strong. The timely use of a bluff greatly increases the odds of victory."

I was mesmerized. I hadn't read the famous book, but I knew it was written in 400 BC.

"Ming and Guo were bluffing because they're weak. Using the same strategy, you'll want to appear stronger than them even if you don't feel like it. Only this way, they'll back off. If you let them push you around, they will."

"Thanks for the advice." Even though I just met Lingling, I started to like her already.

"One time, they did something similar to my brother Lu," Lingling said while we were walking out of the building, "except he went overboard and got into a huge argument with them."

Soon after, our small talk took a sharp turn.

"Do you have any siblings? Most people here don't," Lingling said casually.

"No, I'm the only daughter." I continued walking. "Where do your parents live?"

Lingling hesitated, and then her tone changed. "You know this is a school for orphans, right?"

Nobody told me about this. I immediately regretted my question. "I'm sorry," I murmured. "I didn't realize...."

"It's fine. I'm used to this kind of question," Lingling paused, then said, "but some people like to pry on information when it's none of their business."

Even though she probably didn't mean to make me feel bad, I felt awful.

"I know *you* didn't ask, but I don't want you to hear rumors," Lingling looked down at the grass and said slowly. "So...when my brother and I were infants, there was a huge earthquake in our village. They assumed our parents died because nobody was able to find them. We had to be sent to an orphanage."

"I'm sorry." My voice was small. *What should I say?* A lot of orphans from my last orphanage went through various situations involving their parents. After all those experiences, I still didn't know what to say.

After an uncomfortable silence, Lingling walked away without saying bye. I was left standing there alone.

Little by little, my conversation with Lingling began to settle in, slowly awakening the memory that was carefully guarded and deeply buried inside my head for almost eight years.

I was five. My parents took me on our last trip to China. *To finish some business,* as they told me.

One fateful night, I fell asleep alone leaning against a twisted old tree. I woke up with a start to the sight of a stranger with a shaved head and dressed in a long yellow robe.

"Hello Cassidy. I'm Monk Taiyuan," He spoke softly in accented English.

I quickly scooted away from him.

"I'm very sorry to tell you…your parents have died," Monk Taiyuan said gently, looking into my eyes.

Shocked and mind-blown, my whole world fell apart just like that. I bawled my eyes out. The next thing I remember was Monk Taiyuan taking me to an orphanage in Beijing.

Monk Taiyuan visited me often. At first, I was cold to him. My five-year-old mind thought of him as someone who took me away from my home instead of who kept me safe. I asked Monk Taiyuan about my relatives in Italy, but he said he couldn't find them. I begged to be sent back to anywhere in Italy, but he said it couldn't be done. The reason for that…I'm not sure if he ever gave me a clear reason or if I understood it. Maybe people hate explaining things there.

Later, I realized that Monk Taiyuan had nothing to do with losing my home in Italy and I shouldn't be mad at him.

THE UNTOLD TRUTH OF CLUB 門神

I slowly started to accept him, and we became closer after he introduced me to a game called Mahjong.

Eventually, I got used to living in the orphanage. I ended up liking the people there for the most part, although I stood out from the rest with my brown hair, blue eyes and light-toned skin.

As far as why I moved from an orphanage in Beijing to a boarding school in Southern China is a mystery to me. Fast forward to the day of my thirteenth birthday, which was ten days ago. Monk Taiyuan came to visit me at the orphanage as usual.

"Happy birthday, Cassidy," he said with a glum smile. "Now that you're thirteen, you need to be transferred to a new school in southern China called Paiya Boarding School. It's in the Paiya Mountain."

"WHAT? WHY?" I asked in disbelief. This was the last thing I expected on my birthday. *Surprise! Your birthday present is to live in a completely different place that you know nothing about!*

"It's a long story," Monk Taiyuan said as if he was expecting my question, "which I don't have time for right now. You still have a week before leaving. I'll explain when I come back in a few days."

I didn't want to move, but it seemed like I had no choice even though I wasn't given a reason. Adding to the confusion, one of the workers misunderstood the date. I ended up being sent on a train ride the very next day, but not before tearful farewells to some workers and friends whom I grew up with. Worst of all, I didn't get to say goodbye to Monk Taiyuan.

I came back to my room. Mei was carefully transplanting her small plants into larger pots. Not in my greatest mood, I slumped down on my bed and began writing in my purple diary. I haven't mentioned my diary yet, have I? Well, I've always enjoyed writing and have been keeping up with diaries since I was ten. Recently I've been writing about mysteries surrounding me and trying to make connections between them. I figure I would have a good laugh about my many old theories once I find out the truth.

"Cassidy," Mei said while examining her plants, "my friend Bo Chen is coming back tomorrow. You should meet him. He and I have been friends since the Qing Dynasty!"

"Sure." I chuckled. "What is he coming back from?"

"A three-week trip."

I was surprised that students were even allowed to do that. *What does he do on a three-week trip?*

I'll have to ask Bo tomorrow. Maybe it'll lead to something.

CHAPTER 4:
THE BIG REVEAL
November 15 (Thursday)

Before the morning class, Mei stood by the door chatting with a short boy with bushy black hair and bushy eyebrows, wearing a yellow sweatshirt.

"Oh, Cassidy, this is my friend Bo Chen!" Mei grabbed my hand, full of delight. Bo smiled at me.

"Hi, Bo. How was your trip?" I asked.

Out of nowhere, another girl called Mei. Mei said it was her best friend Yi Han and they needed to discuss an urgent recycling issue at our school. Mei rushed to Yi, leaving me with Bo.

"Yeah, I did." Bo continued our conversation, looking up at me. "You must be new. You're pretty tall for a ten-year-old."

What? Ten? Is that an insult? I don't think it is, but why did he say I'm ten?

"I'm thirteen." I corrected him.

> "What?" Bo looked taken back that someone could be at the age of *thirteen*.

"Yes, what about you?" I supposed all the new students here were ten-year-olds.

"Thirteen too, but I've been here since ten," Bo added casually. "I thought all Menshens are sent here once they turn ten. I wonder which god was thinking of it?"

What...what did he say? I was speechless. Bo said it so lightly that I thought it had to be a joke.

I'm pretty sure Menshen (門神) means door god. If Menshens are sent here once they're ten, and everyone is sent here at ten, does it mean the entire school is full of door gods? I don't think I'm a door god. I wouldn't be surprised if door god has a different meaning at this school, but why did Bo ask which god sent me here?

I barely knew how to describe the amount of confusion I had. If this was on a scale from one to ten, it would be a hundred. "Wh-what's a Menshen?" I asked nervously once I found my words.

Bo tilted his head at me, with the same amount of confusion. "Well, don't you know why you're here?"

"No." I looked at him wide-eyed. *If there is a reason, nobody told me.*

"You do go to this school, right?"

"Yes," I murmured. *Obviously, I'm standing right here at the entrance of the school.*

Bo looked at me with horror on his face. "Excuse me for a moment," he said, then slipped into the not-so-crowded crowd of students, leaving me at the mercy of my own thoughts.

Gods, Menshen, Menshen, gods... those words repeated in my head. Any conspiracy theory that I came up with was immediately thrown out the window. They were nothing even close to this. It's like everything I knew in the world collapsed, and then some aliens came in and rebuilt it after a single conversation.

Only the sound of the bell snapped me out of my trance. I reminded myself to ask Mei about it, as I usually do.

I didn't even try to block off my mind-wandering during the class. It would be pointless because this was the only thing I could possibly be thinking about! The class couldn't have felt any longer. Imagine trying to sit through a history lesson after someone told you THAT!

As soon as the class was over, I made my way to Mei, knocking down a chair or two in the process.

"Mei!" I shouted just loud enough so she could hear me. Mei stopped so suddenly that I thought she was going to fall over. "After you left, Bo talked about Menshens and gods. Do you know anything about it?"

Mei stared at me with her mouth open, apparently trying to comprehend what I said. "I don't. What's even a Menshen?" Mei laughed awkwardly.

"Mei, I know you know something. Does it have anything to do with the after-school club?" I was reluctant to believe her.

"Oh, well that was…was just…" Mei sighed, looking frustrated. She walked away while pulling her braids. "Talk to me during lunch."

My mind started to spin. There were endless possibilities of what Mei was going to tell me. I had no other option but to endure hours of classes for the answer to a secret that had been rigorously guarded.

Classes couldn't have been any slower. It was finally lunchtime. I quickly finished pork fried noodles, which I couldn't even remember the taste of. I anxiously waited at the cafeteria while scanning the room.

"Cassidy." Mei finally approached me. "Are you ready?"

I agreed instantly and followed. Mei checked every corner we turned and paused occasionally as if listening for something.

We turned to a quiet hallway with a door in the center of the back wall. I immediately knew where we were going. I remembered this door because it was constantly closed and had a small touchpad next to it.

Mei punched in eight digits on the keypad. Only the first four digits were shown on the keypad, *9888*. The rest of the numbers became invisible as she punched.

Mei gave me a mysterious smile as she opened the door, revealing a large stone staircase going down, gently illuminated by lights overhead. I followed her in anticipation. Each of our footsteps echoed. My heart was thumping in my throat. At the bottom of the stairs was a flat surface with another double door. Mei pushed it open to reveal an underground world.

Our school itself is plain white with limited decorations, but beyond the double door is a space the size of a mall with lush colors and fancy materials. In the center of the glimmering dark wood floor was a beautifully carved-out marble dragon. Dark red pillars are situated between doors covered with gold-accented paintings. Statues lining the wall were inscribed as god or goddess of…, but I didn't linger on the names because there was so much to take in.

Nobody else was around. I stood marveling at the newly discovered hidden treasure. I could stay there all day.

"Welcome to Club 門神!" Mei said while I was in a daze.

THE UNTOLD TRUTH OF CLUB 門神

"Club door god? Are you a god?" I asked in disbelief as I was digesting everything around me.

"No, we're not gods." Mei laughed light-heartedly. "We die like mortals. We're threshold guardians or Menshens of gates and doors. We're here to guide good into the gates and evil out."

"How?" I couldn't take my eyes off the surroundings for a second.

"With different types of powers. Principal Jiang will have to explain this to you." I thought it was her signal to stop asking questions, although I've only asked two.

I took it all in while we toured. I loved what I saw. Mei pointed to different doors and explained the after-school classes and what they do. She stopped by a large door labeled "The Underground Library".

"Fun fact. In the Qin Dynasty, Emperor Qin Shi Huang (秦始皇) ordered a massive amount of books to be burned around 213 BC. Bo hates him by the way. As a result, modern-day humans no longer have some of the knowledge. Luckily for us, a demigod secretly took a copy of all the books before they were burned. Our school kept them in the Underground Library. To this day, only a few of them are missing."

"Wow," I said in wonder, which has been my response for almost everything around here.

"All statues represent different gods." Mei started to walk again, sounding more and more like a tour guide. "There's one class for each grade and about thirty students in each class," she said as she pointed to the classrooms.

We reached one end of a hallway. The farthest wall was covered in golden plaques. Some were blank, others with names inscribed.

"Mei, what is that?" I snapped out of my daze.

"Oh," she said with her tone dying down, "well, when Menshens protect gates, we may lose a few...." Mei trailed off.

A few? I stared at the dozens of plaques and murmured, "So all these Menshens..."

"Have perished. These names are from the past century."

It was only then I realized how dangerous a job Menshens have. The gods whisk them away when they turn ten and force them to put their lives on the line.

After a long pause, I asked, "Mei, if you could make a choice between living a normal life or being a Menshen, what would you choose?" I blurted out before I could stop myself.

"I guess I would still want to be a Menshen," Mei said. "Sure, it can be dangerous, but Menshens have a job to guard. We believe it's an honor to protect doors for good. You know, before Menshens are sent here at ten, we are given a choice. If anyone declines, the god who gives the power takes it back, and this person is free to live a normal life."

I wonder how fair it is. It probably isn't hard to persuade ten-year-olds to put in years of service. I bet most kids are sold right at the word, *power*. Then again, how much fairer can it be? If I were a Menshen, I wouldn't know what to do without knowing the dangers involved.

The bell rang.

THE UNTOLD TRUTH OF CLUB 門神

"Everyone is coming. We should leave now," Mei said while hurrying toward the staircase.

"Wait, are we not supposed to be down here?"

"*You* are not supposed to be down here."

Following Mei closely, I thought of something. *I haven't been given a choice. Why is that? Why was I chosen? What made me different from all other human beings in the world? Moreover, I'm thirteen, not ten.*

We flew down the empty corridors. Once we turned the last corner before the exit, I saw two *people* strolling down the stairs. *Oh no, it's Ming and Guo, the polar opposites.*

I hid behind the cold pillars, with my back pressed against it. So did Mei, one pillar away from me.

"Do you really think we can't see you, Cassidy?" Ming said. He must be rolling his eyes.

Feeling embarrassed and silly about hiding, I came out. *Please don't see Mei,* my mind begged.

"Did you magically guess the correct code?" Guo said sarcastically. "You know you're not supposed to be down here."

Remembering what Lingling said about the Art of War, I responded firmly, "Well, no one told me I can't come here."

"Of course, we won't tell you." Ming ridiculed me. "Nobody is going to tell the Mahjong-loving white skin because she'll spill all the secrets we've been guarding for thousands of years, and..."

"...it'll be really awful if Principal Jiang finds out that you snuck in here," Guo said slowly. *I can't stand them. It's like they always finish each other's sentences.*

"I brought her here," Mei uttered, stepping out from behind the column.

"Well!" Ming said in a sing-songy voice, "I guess both of you will be in trouble then."

"What do you want?" I tried to get away from them as soon as possible.

"Isn't it obvious?" Ming said, crossing his arms like he was the almighty.

"Withdraw from the Mahjong tournament," Guo added like he could read Ming's mind.

"What?" I yelled. "Why Mahjong?" Out of all the things, they picked Mahjong.

"We're doing you a favor." Ming shrugged. "You're going to embarrass yourself anyway. A white skin playing Mahjong?" They both laughed.

I hated it. I hated that they were making me choose, but I knew my answer. "Fine," I scoffed. "I'll withdraw." I would never get Mei in trouble for something that I asked her to do.

Mei gave them a side-eye, as if they were a piece of gum stuck to the bottom of her shoe. She grabbed my hand and blurted out angrily, "Let's go!"

In the evening, I was back in my room jotting down my thoughts in the diary. I have a small part of the puzzle put together, but still a long way from making complete sense of it all. Menshens are blessed to protect doors... is all I knew. *Can I join the after-school club? Is Mei going to be in trouble?* Those were only a couple of the hundred questions I had. Well, I have a meeting with Principal Jiang first thing tomorrow morning, so I'll ask my questions then.

"Cassidy!" Mei pushed the door open and said abruptly, "You can still play in the Mahjong tournament."

"What?"

"I already told assistant Principal, Ms. Wu, about taking you to Club Menshen." Mei's voice was stern. "She scolded me, but I'd rather that than you giving in to Ming and Guo."

I smiled, grateful that Mei went to great lengths so I could compete, also glad that she stood up to Ming and Gou.

"Thank you, Mei," I said with all my heart.

CHAPTER 5:
TWO PRINCIPALS: PAST AND PRESENT

November 16 (Friday morning)

The first thing I noticed when I entered the principal's office was the much too intense lavender fragrance that made me gag. *Why is it so strong?*

There was a birch desk with an elegant Bonsai on the right, and stacks of papers on the left. Two red banners hanging on the far wall on each side, with a water painting of lavender fields in the center. On top of a bookshelf was a gallon of hand sanitizer. On the right side of the room was a black wooden door.

Sitting on the soft brown leather chair behind the desk was a half-bald, half-grayish-haired man. He had slim eyes, with a stern look on his face. He must be Principal Jiang.

"Hello, Cassidy. Please take a seat. It has been sanitized."

It dawned on me that the lavender scent came from the sanitizer. I sat down across from his desk, anxiously waiting for whatever he was going to tell me.

THE UNTOLD TRUTH OF CLUB 門神

"I'm Principal Jiang. I want to apologize that I couldn't meet with you earlier. I was released from the hospital yesterday," Principal Jiang said, resting his hands on the desk, "It's unfortunate you found out about our school this way. Mei informed the assistant principal, Ms. Wu, of your situation yesterday."

I held my breath.

"Mei is not in big trouble." He reassured me.

I sighed. A weight was taken off my shoulders.

Principal Jiang continued, "I thought Monk Tianyuan had told you about our school before you left the orphanage. I suppose he didn't get a chance because they mistakenly sent you off a week early."

"That's okay. So, after all, you didn't ask everyone to keep the secret from me?"

"No," Principal Jiang said. "In fact, I'm going to rectify it right after our meeting. It is taught here to keep Menshen a secret at all costs to avoid incidents where it could be revealed. People believe you are not a Menshen so the teachers must have changed your schedule to prevent you from joining the after-school club. It could've been avoided if I wasn't in the hospital."

I nodded. *Yeah, it explained my confusion.*

Suddenly, Principal Jiang burst into intense coughing. He turned his face away and put a hand over his mouth, trying hard to contain it. After the coughing finally eased, Principal Jiang cleared his throat and reached for his super-sized teacup. Just when he picked up the cup, his hand began to make involuntary jerky movements, almost spilling the hot tea on the desk.

Is he okay?

Eventually, the jerky motion stopped before Principal Jiang was finally able to take a sip of his tea. "Do you have any questions?" Principal Jiang asked, ignoring what just happened.

"Yes! How do kids become Menshens?" I refocused myself.

Principal Jiang paused for a few seconds, looking like he was pondering the best choice of words. "After humans are born, their brain cells are rapidly developing. Right when infants are turning two, the neurons in their brains are at such a stage that they are most receptive to absorb external forces, such as blessings from a god. Only at this time, the god is able to transmit some of his powers to make this child a Menshen."

Principal Jiang continued as I tried hard to follow him using my limited knowledge of biology. "Gods only pick orphans, so that their parents won't interfere. Once these children turn ten, they are sent to a Menshen school like ours to be trained. Only this way, they are able to gain the special powers blessed from the gods, in addition to other powers they may choose to obtain."

"Do humans have to be blessed at two in order to become Menshens? What if they're older?"

"Precisely at two, on their birthdays. If they are older, their brains will no longer be capable of receiving external signals from the gods."

"Can humans be trained if they aren't Menshens?" Questions were rolling off my tongue, one after the other. I was finally getting the answers I wanted after what felt like forever.

THE UNTOLD TRUTH OF CLUB 門神

"Every human is born with some powers that run in their blood," Principal Jiang explained patiently. "When Nuwa created humans, she used a form of power to make the first group. That part of power stayed in humans and was passed down genetically from generation to generation. That's why humans can also be trained, but only when they are a little older. To be exact, starting at the age of thirteen, like you. Through training, humans are able to gain some of the powers, but to a much, much lesser degree than Menshens."

"Okay." I was still trying to digest all that I heard. "Am I allowed to join Club Menshen then?"

"Of course!" Principal Jiang leaned forward from his chair and emphasized. "Remember, you can't tell any human that Menshens exist, because we must keep the powers among ourselves to make it exclusive and more effective. We must keep our existence as discreet as possible at all costs."

"Sure." I still had a burning question on my mind, so I asked bluntly, "Principal Jiang. About what you said before...Menshens come here for training, but why am I here if I'm not a Menshen?"

"You're an exception." He tapped his fingers on the desk in slow motion.

"Huh, why?"

"Good question." Principal Jiang got up from his chair before I had a chance to ask further. "Now you must go. I will inform the teachers and students of your status immediately."

A rule of thumb:

A teacher should never tell a student it's a "good" question, without actually answering the "good" question.

Principal Jiang walked me to the door. Just when he put his hand on the doorknob, his hand started jerky movements again. The next thing I knew, Principal Jiang had another coughing fit. His face turned slightly blue and then he collapsed.

"Principal Jiang!" I screamed.

"I…I…can't…breathe," Principal Jiang murmured with short and shallow breathing, lying on the floor with a hand over his chest.

My heart was pounding so hard that it shook my entire body. "I'll get help!" I yanked open the door and bolted out of the room. I screamed for help. I busted into the next room, but nobody was there. It was still early in the morning.

"Ms. Wu!" I shouted after spotting her entering the building.

"Cassidy, is something wrong?" Ms. Wu asked softly.

"Principal Jiang can't breathe! He's in his office!"

Without a second of hesitation, Ms. Wu dashed toward me. I had never seen her run so fast. Ms. Wu quickly handed me a phone and yelled, "Call 119 and lead them here!" Then she headed straight to the principal's office.

The phone started buzzing until a calm voice came on. "119. What's your emergency?"

"My principal can't breathe!" I ran toward the gate, out of breath.

"All right, we'll send help. What's your location?" The voice was soothing.

"Paiya Boarding School!"

The 119 operator asked me to stay on the phone while waiting. I couldn't keep myself still. I was shaking, pacing back and forth behind the gate waiting for the ambulance. There aren't any signs for the back roads leading to our school for at least a few kilometers.

What if it comes too late? How long can Principal Jiang stay alive without help?

Finally, the blaring sirens followed by a small ambulance emerged from the forest's trail.

"Where is he?" A group of paramedics carrying a stretcher and bundles of supplies rushed out of the vehicle, huffing and out of breath.

I shouted, "Follow me!" I led the way like the wind until the familiar lavender aroma emerged. "He's here."

The door was open. Inside was Ms. Wu on her knees hooking up a tube to Principal Jiang's nose. The tube was connected to a portable container labeled *Oxygen*.

"We'll take it from here. Wait outside." One of the paramedics said to me while entering the room.

I stood alone squeezing my hands together so tight that my knuckles turned white. The paramedics kneeled down, performed CPR, and gave Principal Jiang a shot with a long-needled syringe. They waited until he looked a little better before they hoisted him up onto the stretcher and left swiftly.

I sighed with relief.

"Thank you, Cassidy," Ms. Wu spoke to me softly. "Principal Jiang probably should have stayed in the hospital a little longer. Now if you're lucky, you can still have a few minutes of breakfast."

My steps were sluggish from exhaustion. I heard the loud noises before I even entered the cafeteria. The crowd was going wild.

"Cassidy! Did you hear the ambulance?" Lingling called to me, shell-shocked.

"Yeah, I did."

"I heard it was Principal Jiang again."

"Again?"

"Yep. A few weeks ago, he was sent to the hospital by an ambulance after spending only one month on the job," Lingling explained.

"One month? He took the job after school had already started?"

"Well, our school needs an authority figure. In addition, Principal Jiang needs to get used to the principal role before he represents us at the annual principal conference."

I gave Lingling a confused look.

"Oh, principals from schools like us come here to meet once a year. Since our last principal died...."

"DIED?"

"Well, assumed dead. All we know is that Principal Song went hiking one day and never came back. We don't know what happened since his body was never found. We thought maybe some wild animal got to him."

"That's horrible," I uttered.

"It is, but our school already did everything possible with rounds and rounds of searches. Let's hope we won't need a third principal this year." Lingling looked at her watch and said, "I got to go."

"Oh, Lingling. I meant to say sorry about my question at the pond yesterday."

"No worries. See you later at the club!" Lingling waved and strode down the hallway.

CHAPTER 6:
THE AFTER-SCHOOL CLUB
November 16 (Friday noon)

"...last time when he was sent to the hospital, he had pneumonia," Bo voiced at the lunch table.

"I thought Principal Jiang had Huntington's disease?" Mei took a bite of tofu.

"He does. Pneumonia is a common complication of the disease at its advanced stage."

Huntington's disease doesn't sound good. I'll have to look it up... but only if I can access the computer again. Our dorm has only one of them and everyone is always hogging it.

"Ummm...Bo, what happened after you left yesterday?" I wanted to change the mood. No more speculations about me, because Ms. Wu had notified everyone of my status on behalf of Principal Jiang.

"Oh!" Bo said. "After I left, I told Mei you weren't a Menshen. She said everyone already figured it out."

"No one knew why you were here though," Mei inserted.

"I suggested erasing your memory...." Bo continued.

"Erasing my memory?" I almost choked on the rice, realizing what happened to me the other day.

THE UNTOLD TRUTH OF CLUB 門神

Mei explained, "One time, Lingling's brother accidentally dropped a scroll in the cafeteria. You saw something on it when you walked by. I panicked and erased your memory for ten minutes."

"If you were going to tell me anyway, why did you erase my memory?" I blurted.

"I never meant to tell you, Cassidy! I wasn't supposed to." Mei frowned.

"It's our standard protocol to erase someone's memory whenever the secret gets out. We don't have other options...." Bo said in a rational tone.

"Alright, I understand. I'm sorry." I backed down.

With the mood dampened, Mei continued the story, "I explained to Bo the rule of Meng Po, which he forgot. Cassidy, in case you don't know, Meng Po is the goddess of forgetfulness. The rule is that you can't use the spell on the same person twice."

"The one thing I forgot," Bo murmured. "By the way, I was gone for three weeks. I have an excuse."

"Yeah, but you won't have *that* excuse anymore," Mei claimed. "Actually, if I knew ahead of time that you told Cassidy about Menshens, I could've come up with an excuse!"

"I don't think you could've." Bo chuckled, lighting the mood.

We laughed, even Mei, who had to admit she was pretty bad at making excuses.

"The club starts in ten minutes," The speaker announced.

I was practically shaking from excitement. Apparently, the Fight class was very important because it was twice as long as usual classes. The classroom was blank white except a poster advertising for the Mahjong tournament on the wall. At this point, the news of Principal Jiang had already spread throughout the school like a wildfire. Almost every other word spoken was *Jiang*.

Mei told me to line up against the wall with everyone else. A teacher with sleek short black hair walked in. It was Ms. Fan. She beckoned us outside the classroom and led us down the hall.

I don't know how you can have a field underground as large as this one. Then again, nothing makes sense the past few days. This field was the size of a soccer field, with random trees three stories tall, and a meter wide. Vines were hanging down like ropes. This place looked like a jungle.

"Why..." I asked Ms. Fan.

"Raise your hand!" Ms. Fan scolded with a cold stare. "Without discipline, nothing can be accomplished!" She sounded and looked like a drill sergeant.

"Sorry," I said quietly, feeling small. I raised my hand this time. "Why are these trees here?"

"They're for coverage," Ms. Fan said in a fast monotone. "You need to learn about your surroundings rapidly and adapt to them. If you don't, you'll never become a good fighter. The trees can transform into towers, obstacles, or nothing."

After that, Ms. Fan instructed us on aims, strategies and tactics with such precise details. I felt like my head was about to explode. Her being a faster talker didn't help. Finally, Ms.

Fan snapped her fingers and yelled to the class, "Now, get ready!"

The trees instantly morphed into moving targets, which surprised me because the trees were humongous. In less than a minute, spears, arrows, and small axes were flying through the air from each lane. The targets kept moving across the field slowly, then became faster and faster, until it couldn't decide on the speed and became completely random. I was thrilled, feeling like I was in an ancient war movie.

Ms. Fan handed me a spear, repeatedly fixed my posture, position, angle, and taught me about motion and timing.

"Is this right?" I was about to throw the spear.

Ms. Fan shook her head. "I told you! Bring your elbow up!"

I raised it a little higher.

"More!" She stepped closer and nudged my elbow. "Now throw."

I felt as stiff as a stick, throwing the spear at a still target. The spear landed a meter away from the red circle on the target. I didn't expect to hit it, but I didn't expect it to be that far away. After numerous tries, I was afraid Ms. Fan was going to lose her patience with my many mistakes.

At one point, my spear came close to hitting a target, missing by a centimeter. Granted my target wasn't moving, and other students were able to hit moving targets.

"You're worse than the ten-year-olds," Ms. Fan criticized me.

I was starting to feel a little better about the last throw, but my satisfaction was quickly demolished. I kept throwing and Ms. Fan continued to correct me every single time. After possibly my worst throw yet, Ms. Fan sighed, "Why are you even here? You're not a Menshen."

It hit me hard because it was the exact question I was constantly asking in my head. I made a promise that I'll come back to practice *until* I prove myself to Ms. Fan.

Spell Class was next. I was determined to do better in this class, even though half of my excitement for the day was diminished. What I didn't know was that this class had only three ten-year-olds. It bothered me because I was the oldest and tallest among all, which made me stand out even more.

Mr. Peng entered. He was the history teacher in the morning.

"Your teacher, Mr. Wang, left for an expedition," Mr. Peng announced. "He won't be back for a while, so I am your teacher for now."

"Mr. Wang is my favorite teacher," a tiny girl sitting next to me whispered in my ear with a radiant smile. She has big eyes, rosy cheeks and a flower clip on her hair.

I smiled back.

"Onto today's lesson." Mr. Peng started. "Remember, power is simple enough to understand but difficult to do. Today, we will continue to learn the easiest one, the fire power."

Someone made an apparent entrance to the classroom. He has a crew cut and a noticeable pointy nose. We call it 朝天鼻, which means "sky-pointing nose" if translated word for word.

"Ah, Ke. I thought we were missing someone," Mr. Peng said with a strict glare. "Why are you late?"

"My dog...ate my...homework," Ke said, his eyes looking down.

The three ten-year olds chuckled at the overused "joke". I could tell Ke is definitely not a teacher's pet type of person.

"You don't have homework for this class or a dog. Now sit down," Mr. Peng said firmly, turning his head to continue.

"I do." It was Ke.

"You do what?" Mr. Peng snarled and turned again.

"Have a dog."

The class chuckled again, louder this time. Mr. Peng tilted his head and sighed.

"It's true. His name is 狗子." Ke insisted.

狗子 (Gǒuzi) is a casual way to say dog in Chinese, like "doggy" in English. Someone named a dog "doggy". What a real genius.

"But Gouzi is a stray dog." A little voice came from somewhere in the classroom. Now the whole class burst out laughing. Don't forget these were ten-year-olds. I remembered Mei told me about a stray dog roaming around our school and everyone loved it. It must be Gouzi.

"Please, quiet down," Mr. Peng said with a disapproving glare, cutting off the laughs. "Since Cassidy is new, I'll do a brief introduction. The fire power does not actually create fire but provides warmth. The god responsible for this power is a peaceful god. So in a way, it's the safest one to learn. Remember, the more you practice, the warmer it gets."

"Can you hurt someone with it?" The rosy-cheeked girl next to me asked. Mr. Peng paused, not sure if this was a joke or an actual question.

"Would it be a spell if it couldn't hurt anyone?" Ke again.

"Actually, not *all* spells hurt people. Ke, you old wisecracker," Mr. Peng shook his head and said. "Anyway, you are all capable of taking on bigger challenges. This one may seem easy, but it is meant to be easy. Anything after this will not be so. I say learning this spell first will be your best bet. This way, your body will have a chance to get used to how spells work."

Mr. Peng took a few steps forward and continued. "One last note for precautions. You may perish from practicing powers. Sometimes students get so scared that they become paralyzed, and forget to do the one most important thing." He paused to emphasize. "To open their eyes. Remember, as long as you open your eyes right before it's too late, you will not die." He talked to us as if he was giving a lecture about running in the gym, not a life-or-death situation.

Two pieces of puzzle in my brain snapped together. It felt like so long ago when I heard it at the lunch table, but now it makes sense why it was such a big deal if someone forgot to open his eyes.

"You will know someone dies from practicing when you see a diamond-shaped black mark on their forehead," Mr. Peng said. "It is an imprint on their rotting skin through their skull."

I felt a chill on my spine.

"Now everyone, close your eyes and hold out your hands," Mr. Peng instructed us.

I did what I was told, before hearing Mr. Peng's voice again. "Relax your hand, Cassidy. It shouldn't be so stiff. Now imagine a fire burning."

"Wait!" It sounded like the rosy-cheeked girl next to me.

THE UNTOLD TRUTH OF CLUB 門神

"Yao Yao, I have told you this already. Cassidy, this is for you too," Mr. Peng said in a mesmerizing voice. "When you try to imagine a small fire, you see a locked door. That's because the god or goddess knows your intention, so they provide this door first. Now you must find your own way to unlock the door in order to start the task. This part I cannot help you with. It's the easiest part, but it helps you to think outside the box. Remember, everyone's door is different."

Slowly, the darkness started to morph and details became clearer. I saw a messy, dark room with a basic wooden door twice the size of me. At first, I imagined trying to unlock it by finding a key, but I couldn't. Then I picked the lock with a thin stick. That didn't work either. After many tries, I simply wedged a stick through the narrow crack.

Surprisingly, the door unlatched. I was relieved and forgot for a second that I had to complete a task. I peeked and noticed a fire about ten times the size of a candle flame in a dark room. I decided to open my eyes to ask, not wanting to do anything wrong.

"Mr. Peng, I unlocked the door. What's next?"

"Well, Cassidy. Here's the harder part. You must carefully obtain the power by letting *'it'* give you its power after completing a task. *'It'* can look inside your head, see your fears, and pick one. *'It'* will choose a different fear each time you try, that is if you attempt again. I know this may sound confusing."

No, it doesn't. It sounds like "it" wants to scare me to death.

"Remember you need to convince *'it'* that you should be able to have its power." Mr. Peng explained, "It's harder for humans because most gods don't take humans seriously. This god isn't like that, so it shouldn't be too big of a problem for you."

Great. I closed my eyes, again. I saw the dark room once more with the fire. *How can I convince "it"? Am I supposed to talk to "it"? Who is "it"?*

"Uh, Mr. Fire man?" I said out loud to no one in particular. The fire glowed brighter. Suddenly, a man stepped out. I jumped back.

"That works every time." The man let out a deep laugh. "I'm Zhurong, as you must know."

"No, I don't." I paused to process the first sight of a god in my head. Zhurong has a thick black beard, with eyes sticking out.

"I am the god of fire," Zhurong said slowly as if explaining a complex math equation.

"Nice to meet you, Zhurong. What do I do now?" It was an unusual experience to be with a god, to say the least.

"Newcomer...Huh. Really! Thirteen years old human." Zhurong swatted away my question.

My head tingled with pressure around it. Maybe he was looking inside my head to pick out my fear. I felt self-conscious. After a few minutes of Zhurong murmuring words, I decided to ask again.

"So, what do I do now?" I tried to sound more confident this time.

"If you look behind, you'll see a forest with a path that leads to a place two hundred meters away." Zhurong said blandly, "There are some matches. You'll have to figure out what to do from there."

"I'll start now."

THE UNTOLD TRUTH OF CLUB 門神

There was a bunch of wildlife along the trail, with birds flying overhead, and rabbits hopping across a narrow path. It was weird. I could still feel my eyes closed and the chair I was sitting on. Yet, I could hear the sounds, and feel the dirt path beneath my feet.

Soon, I saw an open space among the woods. A rock at the side, with a matchbox on top of it. *Strange, aren't gods at least thousands of years old? Why do they use matches?* Next to it were two ancient stone archways facing each other.

I picked up a match from the box, skimmed it along the black part then it became ablaze. The flame caught up to about the size of a grass blade. If the flame was green, I might not have seen it.

Seconds later, the flame grew taller in an instant. I jumped and dropped it out of my hand. I fell backward from the burst of fire. It was a meter taller than me when I sat up from my fall.

After I got up, the fire grew with me, keeping steadily a meter taller and a meter wider on each side. It seemed so real that I could feel the heat. The fire started burning along a path connecting the two arches.

There were more matches, but it wasn't obvious what I needed to do next. I looked down at the matchbox and noticed a lightly engraved picture. It looked like a fire, and next to it was a human walking straight toward it.

What do I do? Walk through the fire? My mind kidded. The longer I was thinking, the more it made sense. It was like two little voices arguing in my head.

Voice one: I really don't want to walk through the fire. Even though I need to succeed in this quest, I don't want to die. That might not even be the correct thing to do.
Voice two: I should go through it. I won't die, as long as I remember to open my eyes.
Voice one: The fire feels so real. I can feel the heat coming off it!
Voice two: Zhurong wouldn't put me on a quest that's impossible to accomplish.

It was kind of like in cartoons where there's a devil and an angel on your shoulders arguing with each other. But in this case, I didn't know which one was the devil, and which one was the angel.

You might think it isn't that hard. Touch it and see if it's real. Side note: Let me stress, do not put your hand in a fire to prove a point! In the end, I couldn't bring myself to walk through a blazing fire that felt so real. Not aware of any other alternatives, I opened my eyes.

"Were you able to complete it?" Mr. Peng asked. "You came back in time. The class will be over in a few minutes."

I shook my head with embarrassment. I noticed everyone else had their eyes open, whispering with smiles on their faces. They probably completed the task.

"Don't worry. I didn't expect you to finish it on your first try anyway," Mr. Peng said calmly.

"Can I ask you a question?" I had doubts about my ability. "I know Menshens have powers but, what makes them better at doing tasks than humans?"

"Well, Menshens have stronger willpower, which signals their brains to produce high levels of adrenaline. It makes them do risky things more readily," Mr. Peng explained.

"Eventually, bravery becomes part of Menshens' personality, and they will do so out of habit. Most of our newcomers obtained new skills on their first attempt, except a few of them had to try again."

"What do Menshens do after they graduate?"

"Other than keeping the secret among us, Menshens grow up to live normal lives and have families with regular people," Mr. Peng said in a civilized voice. "Some of the Menshens who graduated from this school left and took on greater responsibilities. Some of us stayed and became teachers, also with greater responsibilities."

I thought for a moment. "Hmm...has any human been trained before?"

"No. Humans are not directly blessed with power, so you don't have such high adrenaline levels. Human ancestors received some forms of power when Nuwa created them, but the power slowly decreases when passing down through generations."

Alright, I may be able to learn, but the bad news is that it may take me forever at this rate, or I may never get it right. I was frustrated. I was hoping at least there were precedents of humans mastering the spell, but I guess not yet.

Feeling defeated, I slung my backpack around my shoulder and headed back, as if carrying a heavy weight on my shoulders.

Someone was putting up a colorful poster on the front door of my dorm building. The big bold characters jumped right at me-*CAN YOU WIN? The Pre-Qualification Round is Tomorrow!*

Mahjong? Suddenly my mind was filled with the clinking sounds of cards....

CHAPTER 7:
ONE CHANCE

November 17 (Saturday morning)

A giant mob of students maneuvered into the cafeteria with myself among them. It was the pre-qualification round for the Mahjong tournament. Everyone was loud and ready to crush the competition, like screaming goats and herds of cows willing to stampede *anything* that would cross their paths.

Each player was allowed to play one game, and then the number of tokens would be tallied across the board. Only the top sixty-four players would be eligible to participate in the tournament. Filled with the sounds of cheering, yelling, and clattering of the solid cards on the tables, this place was chaotic. I could barely hear myself think! It's like everyone was playing a game called *"Who can be the loudest?"*.

When the game began and fate started to fall into the cards' hands, I thought back to days when Monk Taiyuan taught me. I focused myself against the distractions and used the strategies every chance I got. *I hope the tournament will be nothing like this.*

THE UNTOLD TRUTH OF CLUB 門神

I won, but I wasn't sure if my score was high enough. I waited anxiously until the last game was finished.

"Attention everyone," Ms. Wu spoke softly over the intercom, filling in for Principal Jiang. "The results are in. Congratulations to those who are selected."

Mr. Peng rolled out a whiteboard with a slew of names. The crowd instantly rushed to the board with countless pairs of eyes scanning anxiously for their names. I was barely able to squeeze myself in.

I made it! I was filled with a surge of excitement and smiled an unbreakable smile. Then suddenly it became breakable....

I felt a sudden pressure on my right ankle while I was walking away from the board. Losing my balance and unable to recover, I fell forward like a tree trunk. With a loud bang, I landed on all fours and a sharp pain shot up my knees.

Still on the floor, I glanced behind me. Surprise (or not)! Ming and Guo again, trying so hard not to erupt in laughter. *I can't believe them!* They pretended they didn't see me and made strange faces, yelling something about getting into the tournament.

I was fuming, almost letting out a cuss. *I swear I'll beat them in the tournament!*

Today, my chore was collecting well water. Yep, we were assigned chores and got paid. I learned that all the water we collected from the wells is stored in water barrels and then pumped to the water tower that supplies our entire school.

Later at night, I headed to the kitchen for a snack. My knees were still bothering me. I was surprised to see the lights on, and even more surprised to see Mei there cooking late at night at super speed. A tray of dumplings and other sorts of food spread out on the counter. The kitchen was small for a place holding a bunch of magical Menshens, I would say. I tapped Mei's shoulder.

Mei spun around suddenly. "You scared me," she said, letting out a little laugh.

"Hi, Mei. I just finished collecting water." I grinned at her food. "It smells amazing! Why are you cooking so late?"

"Well, it's my habit to cook whenever...." Mei paused for a good ten seconds before she said hesitantly, "It's nice to do something I know how to do."

"Sorry to interrupt." Bo strolled down the stairs. "I heard pots and pans having a good time in the kitchen," Bo joked.

"Come sit. I could use some help eating all these foods. You too, Cassidy." Mei brought over a tray of steaming hot dumplings.

"Where did you get this food?" I asked as I pulled out a chair.

"I made it from scratch," Mei stated proudly. "I had to make a bunch of trips to the store to buy ingredients because I kept forgetting one thing or another. I bet I annoyed my friend Yi because I brought her with me." She shrugged.

I picked up a soup dumpling and took a bite. It was like a hot explosion in my mouth. The vegan meat was cooked to perfection and the hot juice was full of flavor.

"It tastes so good! Is it made from soybeans or wheat?" I asked.

THE UNTOLD TRUTH OF CLUB 門神

"Soybeans," Mei said, "I have told you I'm a vegan, haven't I?"

"Yeah, you said you hate to think of animals getting killed," I responded. Of course, I remembered our conversations very well. We are roommates after all. Mei told me it was a little hard being a vegan because not many options were available at the cafeteria. That's why she often cooks for herself, learning from the computer.

"Remember the detective book series I told you about?" Bo said abruptly, absorbed in his own world. "The ending of the first book is such a cliffhanger! I'm so glad I can start the next book now that the geography test is over." Bo waved his arm and accidentally knocked his plate off the table.

"You wasted the food." Mei frowned.

"Sorry." Bo picked it up and said in a pleasant tone, "Mei, how did you do in the test?"

"I'm not good at geography." She tensed, then let everything out. "I can't remember places, names, or whatsoever. One question is to name three of the oldest cities along the Yellow River. I couldn't even think of one."

"The Yellow River caused some really bad floods throughout history," Bo went off the track. "I bet the water god, Gonggong, was responsible for most of them."

"But do you know the oldest cities along it?" Mei pressed.

"Sure. Lanzhou, Baotou, Xi'an, Taiyuan, Luoyang, Zhengzhou, ..." Bo continued on. *That's six already! I mean, random knowledge always comes in handy, right?*

"Wow!" Mei interrupted Bo, falsely interested. "How long did you study to memorize all that?" She said bitterly,

"You didn't remember the rule of Meng Po, but you know the Yellow River very well."

"If you study harder, maybe you...." Bo countered.

"Not everyone is as smart as you!" Mei snapped.

"I got to go." After a moment of silence, Bo pushed aside his food and headed upstairs.

"I'll be back." Mei mumbled and disappeared out of the door.

I was left sitting there alone awkwardly, accompanied by the soft sizzling sound of the dumplings in a big pot.

A vague image popped into my head. I was inside a car, and a voice said, "I'll be right back, Cassidy. Don't go anywhere."

I quickly brushed off those thoughts. *Mei will be back.* I sat and waited for her to return.

"Cassidy!" Mei dashed in furiously, yelling and slamming the door behind her. "How can you forget!"

Utterly confused, I got up from my seat. "Forget what?"

"To turn off the water! You said you finished collecting water, but the barrel is completely empty!" Mei's eyes were bulging.

My face slacked. *How could I forget something as easy as that?*

"Did you even check?" Mei continued, "Two people put in two hours of work pulling the water bucket up and down to fill a barrel. Now all of it got wasted because of you!"

"It's my first time."

"It was also the ten-year olds' first time in September," Mei said, "and none of them messed up!"

"You never forget anything before?" I said bitterly, my vision starting to blur.

"Well, I never forget to turn off the water!"

"It's only one mistake," I murmured.

"Do you know how much water got wasted? If you keep forgiving yourself, you'll do it a thousand more times!" Mei threw up her arms in exaggeration.

Silence. The worst silence of all. The kind of silence when you have nothing else to say.

"Oh, you're so perfect then." I stormed out, feeling like a thousand pounds of guilt piled on me.

Under the full moon, a small group of older students were practicing Kung Fu. They were twirling, tumbling, and kicking in the air. Normally I'd stop to watch, but not now. I headed straight to the main building.

I wandered. Reaching the end of the hallway, the warm glow of the library loomed in front of me. I strolled in. Rows of giant shelves, not an inch of the wall was seen. I turned a corner and saw a long soft sofa, which looked so inviting that I practically threw myself at it.

I wish I turned off the water. I know it's a big deal for Mei.

Feeling exhausted after my long day, my eyelids were fighting to stay open. I fell asleep before I knew it.

When I opened my eyes, the sunlight shone directly in my eyes. Suddenly, all the memories from last night emerged. I sprang up from the sofa, flew across the field and dashed up the stairs to my room. I planned out everything I was going to say to Mei.

After taking a deep breath, I opened the door. Mei wasn't in the room. It didn't make sense! Mei is a heavy sleeper, and it wasn't late.

I shut the door behind me, determined to find her. In the pit of my stomach, I had a hunch that she wouldn't come back. *Stop worrying. Maybe she slept in a friend's room. Wherever she was, she would come to the cafeteria to have breakfast.*

Spoiler alert, Mei wasn't at the breakfast. I sat down anxiously at a table where Bo was eating. All the chatters quickly faded into the background. As soon as I caught a break in the conversation, I asked with a slither of hope, "Does anyone know where Mei is?"

"Wouldn't she be in your room?" Someone said.

"No, she wasn't."

"She's probably with Yi," Bo reasoned. "Mei'll be fine."

I knew Mei was strong-minded, but I was still worried. Not that I didn't believe she could take care of herself, but she was in a really bad mood last night. *I need to find her.*

I dashed out, working my way through each classroom and the dorms.

What if Mei is looking for me? Of all the things I know about Mei, she cares about her friends very much despite what happened last night. Suddenly, a frightening thought came to my mind. *Did she go outside the gate? No, I don't think she did, but would she? There's a reason that gate exists.*

I opened the gate and scanned around. It was quiet, only crickets chirping. Suddenly, I heard rustling coming from somewhere. I stepped out from the gate. More rustling, and a tall figure appeared.

I screamed for a brief second, "...Mei?"

THE UNTOLD TRUTH OF CLUB 門神

Mei's shirt and jeans were torn. Her arms and legs were covered in dirt and bruises. She was almost unrecognizable.

"Cassidy! You're safe! Where were you?" Mei's wide eyes got wider.

"The library."

"Oh, I must've overlooked it!"

"What happened to you? I searched for you everywhere!"

"I... fell." Mei hesitated.

"Really?" I was worried but skeptical. It didn't look like a simple fall. *What happened that Mei doesn't want to tell me?* "Mei, what really happened? I promise I won't tell anyone if you don't want me to."

Mei didn't respond for a moment, then sighed. "I guess it's fine if I tell you, because you're not a Menshen."

She pushed open the gate and we started walking back. "After you left, I looked everywhere but didn't find you. I couldn't sleep all night, so I left the gate to the forest right after dawn."

My concerns grew.

"I know I'm not supposed to go outside by myself, but this is the only area I haven't looked." Mei looked back at me. "After an hour of walking, I was about to give up. Just then, I stepped on something that felt like a rock. Suddenly, something large moved around in the bushes next to me. I saw two eyes behind the bushes from a small dragon with a turtle shell. I think it was a Bixi (贔屃).

Mei's voice was shaking, while I held my breath listening. "I got away right before it attacked me. I started running frantically. At one point when I looked behind, the Bixi was only three or four steps away. I wish I had brought my weapon with me. To make things worse, I tripped over something and fell. The Bixi was finally in a perfect position to attack me." Mei took a deep breath and said, "Suddenly, a tree nearby closed itself around the beast."

"What?"

"The Bixi was restrained by the tree branch around its neck and quickly stopped moving." After that, Mei started to sound a little better. "A voice echoed through the forest, making the trees tremble. The voice asked me to follow him. Immediately, all of the plants and trees near me leaned in one direction, so I went that way. The voice told me he is Shujun, the god of agriculture. He blessed me when I was two and I will be much better in his area of power."

"And the power is?"

"He said anything to do with plants, vegetables, crops, trees." Mei cleared her throat, began to repeat Shujun's speech. "Well, this is exactly what he said after that...

'One important rule you must know is that you can't tell any Menshen I met you under these circumstances, or you'll lose your power forever. I regret to tell you I'll never see you again. This is the One Chance I can save your life. Let me give you advice before I go. I know you trust everyone, but don't. You can choose to take this advice seriously or not. Have a good life.'"

"At least now I know I'm able to have power over plants." Mei chuckled a little. I smiled, at least she was feeling better.

"After that, Shujun disappeared. I was still in shock. Eventually, I walked back following the direction he made the trees lean." Mei concluded.

"Wow." I was mesmerized. "Did you know this before? A chance to be saved?"

"No, Menshens only learn about it through their god blessers under life-or-death situations. If they know, they may intentionally put themselves in danger to learn the special power.

"Listen, Cassidy," Mei said seriously, "if you tell any Menshen about this, I'll still lose my power because I told you the secret. The gods know. It may not make sense but they do."

"I promise I won't tell. So, do you mean Shujun won't save you if you're ever in danger again?"

"Right, and it's not 'if'. I'll definitely be in danger again someday. It's all part of the job."

To be honest, I was uncomfortable with how confidential this information was. I did ask though. Then I remembered why Mei was out in the woods in the first place. It may not be a good time for a serious conversation, but I felt it was needed as a friend.

"Mei, I want to apologize for pressuring you to tell me about Club 門神 and wasting a barrel of water. I should've been more careful."

"I'm sorry too. I know it's no excuse, but if I was in a better mood, I wouldn't have yelled at you like that. I did badly on a test, then I got into bickering with Bo."

I hugged her as relief washed over me.

"Just so you know Mei, your grades don't define you," I added. "You don't need to worry too much about it, whether you chose to be a teacher or a door guardian."

Mei smiled. "That's easier said than done. I always get obsessed over a grade. The fact that I'm not good at it doesn't help. I can barely get a B."

"That's still good! You should be proud of yourself."

"You'll not believe how many times people have told me that. It's weird, isn't it?" Mei asked, as if looking for confirmation from me.

"No, of course not. Your brain is just hardwired a little differently than other people. That's never a bad thing. But if it makes you stressed, you should try to change it."

"Okay, thanks Cassidy, I'll try." Mei gave me a smile.

I'll keep my promise to Mei not to tell anyone about One Chance, so I chose not to write about it in my diary for Mei's sake. Now that you heard about this, YOU-CAN-NOT-TELL ANYBODY ELSE, even if you think whom you're telling is human. You never know.

CHAPTER 8:
WISDOM HAS IT ALL
November 19 (Monday Afternoon)

"**D**o I have to go?" A voice emerged from the background. The school was over. Bo and I were standing outside discussing the detective book he was reading.

"Come on! It'll be fun." It was Mei.

I turned around to see Mei dragging another girl wearing a plaid shirt. Her black hair laid over her shoulders behind her pointed ears.

"Cassidy, this is Yi," Mei said, giving me a nervous smile.

"Hi Yi," Bo and I greeted her, followed by a brief silence except the sound of the wind gently blowing through the leaves. Yi didn't respond.

"So, do you want to play Mahjong?" Mei looked around. "We have exactly four people and I have a set of cards."

"Sure! We can use the picnic table there." The thought lifted my spirit.

"You play mahjong?" Yi's eyes darted toward me. "Do you know how?"

"Yeah, I do."

Yi's face scrunched up and finally mumbled, "Okay then."

We sat down and shuffled the cards with the clinking noises cutting into the silence. A feeling of familiarity came to me, which was comforting. Actually, only as comfortable as I could be because Yi kept giving me side glances.

"Yi." I tried to lighten up the mood. "I heard you and Mei help with the recycling at school. How long have you been doing it?"

"Huh." Yi huffed. "Longer than you've lived in China."

"Yi, don't say that!" Mei interrupted.

I wish I didn't ask Yi. I drew my next card, and it was the one card needed to win. "I'm calling."

Yi's eyes widened, as if she was about to roll them but stopped when Mei nudged her. I ignored Yi as much as I could, but I probably caught every single side-eye she gave me. Minutes passed when Yi put down the card I needed.

"I won," I announced, pushing down my cards revealing a clean hand with dots only.

"What?" Yi shouted, "You cheated! How can you build a hand like this?"

I was speechless, feeling insulted. *I can't believe Mei brought her to me!*

"Yi...," Mei groaned, throwing her head up to the sky in exasperation. "Cassidy never cheated, okay?"

"Really?" Yi yelled in anguish, "We've been friends forever! Now you're defending her?"

"Yi!" Bo said, raising his voice, "Ever since Cassidy came, you've been avoiding us whenever we're with her!"

"Is that a surprise? Look at her." Yi gave me another side-look.

THE UNTOLD TRUTH OF CLUB 門神

"What do you mean?" I finally found my words. "Because I'm not Chinese?"

"Yi, stop it." Mei said firmly, "Cassidy is my friend too."

"How can she be? I'll never understand you!" Yi scoffed as she got up abruptly and deserted us.

"I'm sorry, Cassidy," Mei sighed. "I promise she wasn't like that before. I brought her here so she could realize that you're not who she thought you were."

"She thought you were a disgrace to this school and should go back to whatever country you came from," Bo added.

"What?" I blurted out.

"Why did you tell her?" Mei stage whispered.

"I just thought she should know."

The mood dampened. I was upset but that quickly turned into relief now that Yi was gone. I looked down at our table. For one thing, we needed one more person to play Mahjong.

"Cassidy!" It was Lingling walking to us with a boy who looked a bit familiar. "Can you help us with something? This is my twin brother."

"Lu Sun." He pushed up his rectangular glasses. Lu had a long face with a darker skin tone that goes along with his orange sweatshirt.

Lingling glanced at the rest of the table and said, "Hi, Mei and Bo. Nice to see you." I could tell that both of them don't know Mei and Bo very well, like a classmate you know exists but never talk to.

"Sure, Lingling. By the way, we're missing one player. Does either of you want to join us?" I said with hope.

"Lingling can play. I'll watch." Lu stood next to us and cracked an overdone smile.

Lingling sat down on Yi's seat and confessed, "I just started learning Mahjong, so I'm not that good."

"That's fine. So, what kind of help do you need?" I asked.

Lingling rummaged through her backpack and said, "I found this in the Underground Library." She revealed a small piece of paper, with words jotted down in the most beautiful handwriting I'd ever seen. This is my translation:

> *A string of jewels among the seas*
> *Pulchritudinous yet ruthless*
> *White to red then red to black*
> *Everything must fall*
> *Wisdom has it all*

イヤイライケレ

I wanted it to sound poetic in English, so I translated it with a little rhythm, and even found a fancy word I never heard of before (you know which one). You're welcome.

"You found a poem?" Bo asked, perplexed.

"No, it's a riddle, I think," Lingling said, "I was reading the copy of a book series that was burned by Emperor Qin Shi Huang. The fifth book is missing. Inside the fourth book, I found this piece of paper. Have you heard of the legend of One-Armer (独臂人)?"

Bo and Mei nodded.

"One-armer?" I was bewildered.

THE UNTOLD TRUTH OF CLUB 門神

"According to the legend," Lingling explained, "hundreds of years ago, there was a Menshen named Hao who had only one arm. She was the best fighter at our school in centuries. Hao was admired and earned the nickname One-Armer. However, she stole some rare books from the Underground Library and ran far away. Those books were the last copies in the world because the rest were burned by the emperor."

Lu continued the story with a fascinated look on his face. "Hao was caught eventually, but the books she stole were nowhere to be found, still to this day."

"Well, didn't our school make copies of the books?" I asked.

"There are too many books to make copies," Lu added.

"What does One-Armer have anything to do with the riddle?" Mei asked, putting our conversation back on track.

"You see, the riddle was placed in the fourth book, right before the missing one." Lingling started her theory. "Maybe it gives information on where to find the fifth book. Look, there's even an arrow pointing to an area at the back of the paper."

After hearing such a wild theory, Mei and Bo blurted out with a bunch of questions.

"How do you know for sure?"

"Why did Hao put a riddle in the book?"

I stayed silent but mystified.

"Wait, wait, wait," Lingling said, stopping the overlapping chatter. "I know this theory sounds far-fetched. But a legend can transform when being passed down over a very long period, so we don't know how far it's from the truth. Hao could have had a partner for all we know! Maybe her accomplice felt bad and wanted to leave a clue for someone to find the missing books."

Bo squinted, being critical. "But it *was* hundreds of years ago. How come no one found the riddle before?"

Lingling shrugged. "Normally we should tell the teachers, but not yet. My theory might not be true, and we could make a big deal out of nothing. How about we keep it a secret until we solve the riddle?"

"I'll help," I said, sure that even if it doesn't lead to anything, it would still be fun. The rest of us agreed to take a stab at it.

Lingling gave a mysterious smile that reminded me of Mona Lisa.

"Any more ideas, anyone?" Mei glanced at each of us as we started another round of Mahjong. We'd been working on the riddle for an eternity, and it still wasn't going anywhere.

"Who has wisdom? It's not an object?" Lu asked after Lingling recited the riddle one more time. Lu had been standing the whole time, looking a bit bored. His overdone smile was fading slowly.

"*Wisdom has it all* probably means wisdom holds the answer to everything, not who has wisdom," Lingling said, drawing a card.

"What about a string of jewels, like a necklace?" I spoke. "It'd make sense, a little bit."

"Maybe," Bo agreed, "but I think this stuff is mostly a metaphor."

"Yeah, it could be something valuable that's among the sea. Not literally like a jewel," Lingling said.

"Is it a sunken treasure?" Lu asked with disbelief.

"What about the other stuff that's in the sea? Like sea creatures, plants." Bo pondered.

"I'm calling." I was about to win the game. "So, what goes from white to red then red to black?"

Lu looked up, then had an idea. "The clouds. They're white during the day, turn to red during sunset, then turn black at night."

Does it make sense?

"No, rays are light. The light spectrum has seven wavelengths that are visible to human eyes," Bo said. "The clouds are made of tiny water drops, really tiny. They deflect light at seven wavelengths. That's why you see different colors of clouds, similar to a rainbow."

Bo repeats himself a lot, like the words seven wavelengths. I was dumbfounded what he was going for.

"I won," I announced, pushing down my cards. Others groaned. We started another game.

"So does everyone understand what I mean about the seven wavelengths of the light spectrum and the tiny water drops in the clouds? The rays of light...." Bo paused suddenly then murmured, "Sorry I know I said it already. I just wanted to make sure everyone understands."

Yep, at least Bo is aware of his repetitiveness.

"Okay, I mean clouds might work because lightning could be dangerou-," Mei said but was interrupted by Bo.

"Mei, I just told you why it isn't clouds!"

"You did?"

"The clouds technically aren't red, or yellow," Bo said. "Remember white isn't a color. White represents all colors!"

Bo said, finally making sense of part of the riddle. "So, what it says is that it turns anything into red, then black!"

After this spectacular discovery, we were stuck at a seemingly dead end. If I could sigh in words, I would. Repeating a riddle was torturous.

"Like I said, even though clouds are not technically red or black, they look that way!" Lu said for the one hundredth time, defending his cloud theory.

"But it doesn't have a string of jewels!" I exclaimed.

"Well," Lu didn't give up. "Give me a few minutes. I'll come back with an excellent answer!" Lu said, looking elsewhere.

"Fire, maybe." I was thinking out loud. "Fire will ignite anything into red flame, then burn to black. Once it's burned, it'll fall." My fire theory sounded pretty accurate to me.

"And fire can be deadly!" Lingling agreed excitedly.

I noticed there are two types of people based on how they respond to solving a riddle. The first type is hoot and holler (Lingling, Lu and Bo), or whatever it's called in English. I thought owls were supposed to hoot. This is confusing.

The second type shows signs of relief, then slumps down looking weary enough to take a nap at twelve o'clock in the afternoon (Mei and I).

"I'm not saying it's impossible for it to be fire, but hello? Clouds, lighting? It's deadly too!" Lu insisted.

"Let's solve one part at a time. It'll help the rest," I said. "We can also search up what those symbols mean."

"The first line, a string of jewels among the sea...probably means multiple valuable things in a line," Bo said before he called the game. "But how is it connected to fire?"

"Doesn't lightning cause fire sometimes?" Lu held on to his cloud theory.

After that, it was getting a bit boring again. I think today may have ruined riddles for me, at least for a while. Then there was a sudden snap that made everyone jump. Turned out it was Lu who snapped his fingers.

"Before I say it," Lu looked around and said, "is everyone sure it's not clouds?"

Honestly, clouds make sense too, but jewels among the sea? Believe me, I did think about clouds, but it hit a dead end. There are more possibilities with fire, so we said we were sure.

"A chain of islands," Lu said at last.

"Yes! There's fire, so they're islands formed by volcanoes!" I exclaimed excitedly, thinking on the spot.

"I don't think anything else could fit better." Bo acknowledged.

Some of us cheered, and some sighed again.

"Well," Lingling put down a card and said in a false cheery voice, "the last line makes the least sense, *wisdom has it all*. It's not even connected to fire, or clouds!"

"So you *did* hear me," Lu mumbled.

"I won!" Bo grinned ear-to-ear, pushing down his cards. "Anyway, the final clue may come from the unknown characters in the end," He said thoughtfully, ignoring Lu. "I'm going to search up whether they're from some kind of language."

We were stumped at this point. It was impossible to know which language those characters were without any help. The game continued.

"How do you think Principal Song went missing?" Lu asked randomly while looking around, probably bored to death. He was the only person who didn't play the game.

"I still think he got attacked by a wild animal. He probably got eaten so we couldn't find his body," Bo said, drawing a card from the stack.

"No, no, no, no!" Lingling said quickly, moving her hands through the air, "Principal Jiang specifically said NOT to spread rumors, because they were getting out of hand! Someone even said Principal Song was abducted by aliens for goodness sake! We need to listen to the authorities. Lu and Bo. Please stop." Lingling said firmly.

"Fine," Bo and Lu replied in a small voice.

Lu let out a big yawn. His overdone smile was nowhere to be seen. "Let's continue the riddle another day."
We couldn't agree more, as it was getting tiring. After we separated, I made a quick stop in the kitchen of my dorm.

"Cassidy! Cassidy!" A small voice came from the kitchen. It was Yao Yao, the rosy cheeked girl from my spell class. Since we met, Yao Yao liked to strike up conversations with me. I didn't expect to befriend a ten-year old, but Yao Yao was sweet and fun to talk to. It looked like she had been waiting for me for a while.

"Yao Yao?"

"There is something I need to tell you." Yao Yao lowered her voice, cheeks flushing. "Promise me you won't tell anyone. I'd be in trouble."

"I promise," I assured her, worrying more about Yao Yao than whatever she was going to tell me.

Yao Yao looked around to make sure nobody was there, then sighed. "Ming and Guo asked me to do a job."

"What kind of job?"

"Well…." Yao Yao was biting her tongue. "I didn't want to do it but Ming and Guo said I owed them a favor."

My eyes widened. *Yao Yao and the pair? They have absolutely nothing in common!*

"Uh…one time, I fed the stray dog some wild berries that I found in the woods," Yao Yao took a deep breath and said, "Gouzi got really sick. Everyone was worried about it but didn't know why. Ming and Guo happened to see me giving berries to the dog, so they said I owe them a favor whenever they demand it, or they'd tell everyone."

"A favor? Like what?" I was flabbergasted. *They stooped so low to blackmail a ten-year-old.*

"To help them." Yao Yao was dead serious. "They're going to sabotage you at the Mahjong tournament!"

CHAPTER 9:
SHOWDOWN AT THE MAHJONG TOURNAMENT
February 2 (Saturday)

TWO AND HALF MONTHS LATER

Ever since Yao Yao told me about Ming and Guo's plot to sabotage me in the Mahjong tournament, I have been cracking my brain on what to do. On the one hand, nothing will stop me from competing in the tournament. On the other hand, I won't let the pair publicly humiliate me. What makes it tricky is that I can't tell anyone about it because I promised not to expose Yao Yao.

Finally, I thought I had a plan. Will it work? I'm not so sure.

Apart from practicing Mahjong during the last few months, I've been working very hard on my fighting skills. As much as I wanted to say my skills improved drastically and I was amazing, I wasn't. Since my first attempt at the fire spell, I tried two more times and failed two more times. At least, I was able to throw spears much better after spending numerous hours practicing on my own. Actually, I'd say Ms. Fan was impressed by my throw at the last class. She even cracked a little smile. Of course, I'm still not at the same level as other students.

THE UNTOLD TRUTH OF CLUB 門神

Speaking of powers, I was told that Menshens are capable of learning different kinds of powers in addition to what they are blessed with. For instance, everyone is required to learn the fire spell first. Furthermore, Mei is able to cast a spell to wipe someone's memory for ten minutes, like what she did to me. Bo practiced a spell from Chenghuang god so that he can create a shield using his palms when he commands it. I heard Lingling and Lu have some sort of water power, but I haven't seen it.

After Mei's encounter with Shujun, her god blesser, she found out she was capable of obtaining a power to keep living things in their current form. One morning, I woke up to see Mei on her knees at eye-level of one of her plants. Her eyes barely blinked, staring straight at the plant as if she was a teacher giving complex instructions to a student.

"What...are you doing?" I rubbed my eyes, still half asleep. "Ah," Mei jerked her head and blinked forcefully a few times. "I was practicing the spell I told you about."

Quickly becoming wide awake, I grinned with a newfound excitement. "Keeping living things in their current form?"

"Yep," Mei said in a tired voice.

"How does it work? You stare at a plant, and it stays still?" I asked using my layman's terms.

"Well, I have to stare at it for at least an hour," Mei said with a straight face, "until I feel my energy fully reach the plant for the amount of time I wanted. Hopefully, it'll get easier over time."

"Doesn't a plant stay in the same position anyway?"

gradually lean back toward the sun again. I'm practicing to prevent sun-leaning from happening."

"How long will one hour of practicing keep the plant stay still for?"

"Three days based on my research, but it could take longer to practice at first. I get headaches and sore muscles in the process."

"Hopefully, it'll be worth it in the end."

Mei nodded. "Maybe I can use my spell to slow down enemies, but I need to make it work on plants before I try it on animals."

Days passed. Mei kept practicing on her plant. To her amazement, the stem stayed in the same position, with the duration of effect extending little by little each time.

Finally, Mei brought me to the pond to try her spell on a frog. Although it only paused for a nanosecond, we cheered so loud that we scared off the little frog.

With all that's going on, New Year's Eve is getting closer and closer. Mei has been busy helping with the cafeteria staff making plans for the party food. She invited me to cook with her and I gladly accepted.

Meanwhile, my anxiety is growing because it also means the Mahjong tournament is right around the corner. Being fearful that my plan wouldn't work, I go through it in my head over and over.

It has to work.

The day of New Year's Eve finally arrived. Chinese New Year, also called the spring festival because it lasts weeks, is the most exciting holiday of the year. After months' preparation, we couldn't wait any longer.

THE UNTOLD TRUTH OF CLUB 門神

I woke up early in the morning. The sky was gray and the air was damp, but it didn't dampen our mood a bit. I could practically feel the exhilaration in the air everywhere I went. People were running around or busy doing things, wearing their best clothes in red. When I got close to them, they would drop whatever they were doing and scream straight into my ears,

"Happy New Year!"

That was just how excited we all were. Apparently, our school takes pride in having student volunteers run the New Year's Eve party, which is the biggest event at school. It takes place in the cafeteria where volunteers decorate the room and cook the party meals.

"Happy New Year!" I was on my way to the cafeteria when Bo came up to me wearing a red and golden dragon patterned shirt. We greeted each other.

"Guess what? I finally figured out the riddle!" Bo raised his bushy eyebrows so high that they almost reached his hairline.

"Riddle?" I hadn't thought about it in months. In fact, I almost forgot about it. "Oh, you did? Great! What is it?" I said with hope.

"The symbols. I found out what they meant!" Bo uttered while clapping his hands together in excitement.

"Well?"

"I started reading books on cultures and languages whenever I had time," Bo rambled on. "Anyway, according to a website, I found out those words meant 'I hate it' in Japanese."

It could make sense since Japan consists of a bunch of islands.

"But it still didn't make sense because Japan has over six-thousand islands!" Bo read my mind. "I thought the riddle would be more specific, so I kept looking. I started to read books on extinct languages and cultures. Then I found out that in this particular language, it means thank you."

Bo kept going on and on in circles. "Now, this is the confusing part. In Japanese it means I hate it, but Japan has over six-thousand islands. Remember? So, I wasn't sure about '*I hate it*' because..."

"Bo! What language is it?" I was losing patience.

"Sorry, I'm getting to it," Bo mumbled. "The language is Kuril Ainu, which originated from the Kuril Islands. Now hear this out." Bo paused for two seconds for suspense.

This time *I* raised my eyebrows.

"The Kuril Islands are a chain of islands formed from volcanoes! 'Thank you' may just be random words."

"Thank you!" *I mean I'm grateful for his answer. I'm not repeating the words from the riddle.* "Hopefully, the missing books are there."

"Yeah. That would be nice." Bo nodded with a grin.

"Oh, I'm going to the cafeteria." I remembered I was supposed to help Mei cook. "Are you going too?"

"Not yet. I'll see you soon!"

A bunch of students came to the cafeteria, forming a sea of red. Inside, people were busy putting up festive decorations like colorful paper flowers, animals, and symbols. Dozens of red lanterns lined up along the walls. Scrolls of water-color paintings and poems were hung from wooden poles.

THE UNTOLD TRUTH OF CLUB 門神

Some of the students were arranging Mahjong tables, making loud scratching noises as they were dragged across the floor. Sixteen game tables made of dark wood sat in the center of the room with a chair on each side. Underneath the square table top was a small shelf for players to keep their tokens.

I was way more excited for the Mahjong tournament than I let on. I could finally show that I am capable of doing something well. Quite frankly, I love playing Mahjong! The way you strategize each game based on your own cards and opponents' cards by speculating, predicting, taking calculated risks and being right in the end is truly an underrated feeling. Of course, a little luck helps too.

More people came in by the second, loud and with big bright smiles. I joined Mei in the kitchen to cook an absurd amount of food.

Laughing hysterically, a group of students walked in. One of them was Yi, dressed in bright red. As soon as Yi's and Mei's eyes locked, Yi turned her head away. Mei abruptly dropped the vegetables in the strainer and walked to the back door, murmuring something about getting water. Right then and there, someone called *Guilt* punched me in the face. I knew they used to be best friends, but not anymore....

Ming and Guo trudged in, glancing around the entire cafeteria like they were judges. For a second, I thought they came to help. How I got that crazy idea, I don't know.

Suddenly, Ming glanced in my direction. I jerked my head back to focus on seasoning the pork. Over all the noises, I heard the pounding footsteps coming my way.

"It looked better last year." It was Ming's voice.

"Yeah, I hope people at least wash their hands before cooking this time," Guo seconded. Well, I hope that was a joke.

"Can I help you?" I lifted my head and asked before they could say any dumber insults.

"Nothing. We're just checking to make sure you're seasoning it right," Ming said obnoxiously.

Being stared at every move, I felt stiff and uncomfortable. "People are setting up tables over there. You should go help," I said a little more quietly than I wanted to.

"Watch the salt," Guo said with a smirk.

I glanced at the salt bottle I was holding. It was like a waterfall pouring out and forming a small white hill on top of a big chunk of pork I was preparing. Both of them laughed, while I rummaged through the drawers to find a spoon. I slammed the drawer back, scooped up all the salt, and rinsed the meat under running water. *I can't believe I ruined the meat.*

"I guess white people aren't as good at cooking as us." Ming laughed.

The fact that they took anything I was lousy at then generalized to all white people made me feel irritated, but also at loss.

"Try not to mess up Mahjong like that roast pork." Guo snickered.

That was what they did. They came here for less than a minute, but the amount of annoyance they gave me was beyond words. At the word Mahjong, I tensed. I promised Yao Yao I wouldn't tell anyone she informed me of their plot. If the words get out, I'm positive she would never hear the end of it from both.

"Yeah, and don't feel the need to cheat," Ming said.
"You'll lose either way."

Guo seemed to be upset at Ming, mouthing words at him while leaving together. They *really* got under my skin. I went over my plan in my head one more time.

The preparation was finally done. The air was filled with the smell of delicious food. After the last bowl was put down, people started screaming, cheering and jumping around before the event even began!

The space in the cafeteria was maximized with dozens of additional tables and chairs, extending into the hallways. The windows for handing out food were fully stocked and ready to go. The floor was spotless (for now). Shining light from the red lanterns covered the entire space, so bright that I bet it could be seen from hundreds of meters away.

Shortly after, Principal Jiang walked in, partly covering his eyes from the bright lights. After his last health scare, Principal Jiang has been doing much better. He congratulated us on the magnificent job and said the rest of the school was coming as he spoke.

As if on cue, a huge crowd came out of nowhere, like bees bursting out of a broken hive. Principal Jiang picked up a giant bottle of hand sanitizer, stood by the door and sprayed everyone's hands as they entered the cafeteria. Instantly, the aroma of lavender filled the air.

It was an amazing dinner. The food was delicious, even though I took a chance that whoever made the meal washed their hands. Mei, Bo, Lingling, Lu and I sat together eating, joking, laughing and having boatloads of amusement. We became very close friends over the last few months.

At one point, Bo kept rambling on about the zodiacs and it got *really bad*. Finally, Bo apologized and said he has O.C.D.. Of course, it's fine with me. Bo's my friend and that's the way he is.

I never saw so many students and teachers in such a joyful mood and bright smiles on their faces. Cheerful folk music was playing in the background. Many of us began to sing along whenever a popular song was played. Ms. Fan walked around to tap on the shoulder of anyone who was singing on the top of their lungs, followed by a strict glare. In the meantime, Mr. Peng was busy breaking down any potential food fights.

First round -

"Attention please," Principal Jiang said into the intercom, "the first round of the Mahjong tournament starts in a few minutes. All contestants, please take your seats at the designated tables."

People rushed in excitement to get things off the game tables before dumping boxes of Mahjong cards with loud clatters.

I almost jumped out of my seat. My heart was hammering against my chest. I had waited for months, and it didn't seem real. I sat down at my table, noticing every detail around me. The small cracks on the table, and the tiny pieces of food on the once clean floor. Before long, three other players sat down at the same table with me. Everyone was given the same number of tokens to start with.

THE UNTOLD TRUTH OF CLUB 門神

Accompanied by the rumbling sound, Yao Yao rolled out a white board to keep track of scores.

My trance was only broken by the loud clicking noises when the other players started to shuffle cards. We put up cards in rows of eighteen by two. One of us rolled the dice, and the game took off.

Surrounded by layers of onlookers, I felt all pairs of eyes staring at my every move. My instincts guided me through the game. Obliterating fear or nervousness, I was doing something I knew how to do well. I remembered all those times when Monk Taiyuan taught me from a young age, how I got frustrated at first because I didn't know the Chinese characters on the cards, how much I got better over the years, and how I played with other kids and laughed until our lungs hurt.... I don't think I'll ever not miss it.

Drawing every card with the hope that it was the one I needed, discarding each card expecting that no one else would claim it, I played with strategy and techniques I had learned. I got to a point when I only needed one of the two cards to win, a card with eight lines or a sparrow that represents one line. I quickly announced, "I'm calling."

My nervousness crept in. My palms were sweaty, and I could hear my heart thumping as each card was put down and picked up. Until one player held a card close to his face and cringed at it before laying it on the table with a sigh. I was never so happy to see that weird-looking sparrow in my life! I snatched the card as if it were a precious gem I raced to get. I pushed down the rest of my cards and declared with an ear-to-ear grin, "I won!"

Others groaned in defeat, but nothing could stop me from smiling. Two more games were played, with one loss and another win for me. Luckily, I had the most tokens at my table.

In the fifteen-minute break, I felt like I was on cloud nine. My friends came to congratulate me.

After many hugs and praises, Bo concluded as if he was the game official, "*You* are going to the second round!"

Lu tittered and turned to him. "Bo, are you in the second round too?"

"No, I'm not great at card games. I remember facts better," Bo stated proudly.

"I can never understand Mahjong," Lu murmured.

"Lu, did I not teach you how to play?" Bo asked rhetorically.

"I didn't have the patience and the person teaching me got frustrated." Lu glanced at Bo. "All I heard was gibberish coming out of his mouth."

"I can teach you if you want." I offered Lu.

Lu scrunched up his face and said hesitantly, "Maybe...."

Whether he said that to be polite or he wasn't sure, I'm not passing up the chance to spread the wonders of Mahjong.

Second round -

The Bell rang.

"The second round will begin in a moment. All contestants, please take your seats." Principal Jiang announced.

At this round, there were four tables for sixteen players, winners from the first round. I strolled to my table feeling better than ever to play in front of everyone, with a sense of certainty that I could win if I concentrated.

I felt confident, only forgetting one important detail...*Ming.* Once I saw him sitting arrogantly at the same table, a mixture of anxiety and adrenaline washed over me. On the one hand, I couldn't wait to show him my skills, not acquired genetically but through years of practice. On the other hand, I knew I would be hard on myself, not wanting to make any mistakes.

I took my seat as calmly as possible. Ming glanced at me and shook his head as if saying *I can't believe Cassidy made it to the second round.*

Round two started. Despite my best efforts, I lost the first two games. Ming won one of them. I was getting nervous, my fingers tapping rapidly on the shelf under the table. *I have to win, and win big.*

The third game which would determine the winners to advance to the final round commenced. The entire cafeteria was so quiet that you could hear a pin drop. I opened my cards. To my delight, they couldn't be any better! I already got three cards in a sequence and a few pairs. Every card could be put into good use, so it was difficult to give up any of them. Before too long, I got to a point that I was ready to win pending the last card "West".

In a game like Mahjong, you want to remain poker faced until you call it, but the thing that completely baffled me was Ming being the opposite. He laughed at his own cards, snickered whenever someone put something down. Quite frankly, it was getting to me. *Do his reactions mean something or is he playing with our heads?*

I was so lost with Ming's reactions that I didn't notice it was my turn to draw a card.

"Cassidy?" Ming rolled his eyes.

"What? Oh right," I said, slightly embarrassed. As I picked up my card, I quickly scanned the cards that were already on the table. I messed up...*badly*.

I silently kicked myself. Ming had discarded the "West" card earlier, and I was too distracted to notice it. It was the worst low-level mistake I made in the highest stake game I've ever played. There are four "West" cards in a set, which meant only one of them was remaining out there.

Focus! Monk Taiyuan's voice echoed in my head. I brought myself back to reality and concentrated on the game.

I was betting on beating the odds. I picked a card, and it was the "East" card. *Okay, stay focused.* Next, it was a dot. *Alright, next.* Then nine dots. *Come on.* I drew once more and I couldn't believe my eyes. In my hand was the last "West" card! I almost fell out of my chair at the sight of it. I pushed down all my cards and announced excitedly, "I won!"

With a big win in the third game, even though I lost the first two, I still scored the most tokens at my table. I sighed with relief. Ming slammed down his cards and stormed off. The table shook as he knocked the corner of it.

I came back to my friends where I was met with contagious smiles.

"I bet you're going to win the final round!" Bo said without a seed of doubt in his voice.

"You're so lucky you got the last West card!" Lingling grinned.

I was caught off guard. I didn't plan to tell anyone about my error, but I did anyway.

"Oh well, you still beat him." Lu assured me, and the others agreed. They made me feel better about my mistake,

THE UNTOLD TRUTH OF CLUB 門神

but it was like telling a person with insomnia to just sleep. It didn't work that easily.

Now it was down to four players for the final round. Besides myself, it was Guo, Ke, and a student I hadn't met before. While my friends were chatting away, my heart was hammering in my chest ready to burst out any moment. I took deep breaths to alleviate my stress without much success. The image of myself being sabotaged was daunting.

"Cassidy!" Yao Yao sneaked behind me and said skittishly, just loud enough for me to hear, "Ming told me I'm not needed for their plan. Be careful."

"I will. Thank you." I said calmly, not wanting to show any nervousness in front of Yao Yao. I knew she was not needed because only Guo made it to the final round, so Ming would be able to put the sabotage into action....

Final round -

The loud beep that I dreaded came on.

"The final four contests, please take your seats for the last round." Principal Jiang spoke enthusiastically.

The students cheered. Even though the room was the opposite of cold, goosebumps covered my arms. Anxiety creeped up, and my hands started to twitch. All I could hear was the muffled roar from the crowd when I made my way to the table. Surroundings had been cleared out so people formed tight circles around the table.

I squeezed through layers of onlookers. Sitting in the chair, I felt hundreds of eyes watching my every move. Guo sat at the right side of me. The thought of being framed by the pair and facing everyone's disgusted looks was distracting, to say the least.

It turned dark outside. Fireworks started booming. I tried my best to block out all the noises. Two games went by, I won one and Guo won the other. Guo had slightly more tokens than me. *The next game is my last chance.*

The dice was thrown in the air, thumped on the table and rolled to five. I took my cards and erected them in a row. Not a great start...nothing matched, only two cards could be put into a sequence. That was about it. My breath turned shallow. *Of course, now my luck rolls thin. I'm going to lose the final game.*

Ke picked up and put down the first card with a bone shaking clatter on the table. "Best of luck to all of you." He gave a smirk. "But only one can win."

The game to determine the final winner was underway. The air felt cold and crisp, impossible that people had been cheering out of excitement only minutes ago. We stared at each other dead in the eye as if it was a standoff and only one could survive.

BOOM, a loud thud came from the other side of the room, sounding like something heavy crashed on the floor. Everyone craned their necks toward the noise.

It's Ming! He stood next to multiple scrolls that fell on the floor. These were the largest scrolls of poems with heavy wooden cylinders at one end. Since they were only supported by two wooden poles, they were about as easy to knock down as a baby.

"What happened?"

"Is anyone hurt?"

Loud noises broke out. People rushed over to help.

Like a light bulb switched on, I instantly knew this was the start of Ming and Guo's scheme, where one of them would cause distraction and the other one could frame me, as Yao Yao said. She was the backup in case both of them were in the final round. My heart was throbbing in my throat.

Ke and the other player at my table were staring at the chaos around the fallen scrolls, completely unaware of what was about to happen under their noses. According to my plan, I pretended to be distracted while glancing at Guo in the corner of my eyes.

Guo scanned around and snatched two cards from the end of one stack. He silently put them on the shelf beneath the tabletop and slipped them to my side.

A blanket of anger was thrown at me. *He's framing me for...hiding cards!* Not a second too late, I pressed my hand firmly on top of Guo's hand to stop him from incriminating me. Two cards were still under his palm.

Guo froze.

I stared at him and said in a frigid voice, "Excuse me?"

Guo's face immediately turned red and twisted with distraught. He whispered while stumbling on his words, "...please...."

Really, please, *after what he did? He wanted to humiliate me in public. Now he thinks "please" will work?*

Right then, I saw a hint of regret on his face. He was like a rabbit stuck in a dark hole, desperately waiting for a way out. I wasn't so sure anymore....

I gave my hand a quick shove, knocking off the cards under Guo's hand. Two cards hit the floor with a string of distinctive clattering sounds, rolled a few times and landed face up. Both of them were flower cards.

Ke, the other player, and a few people nearby turned their heads to the noise.

"Guo, you dropped these." My voice was a bit louder than usual.

"Oh, I could use those bonus cards!" Ke said jokingly.

The people nearby quickly returned their attention to the fallen scrolls. Guo looked at me, with his mouth open.

"Are you going to pick them up?" I said to Guo, with a smidge smile of victory.

"Yeah…." Guo's voice cracked. He picked up the two cards with a shaking hand, then put them back on the stack.

I took a deep breath. *This is it*. I prevented the sabotage. *But what if I was a moment too late to stop Guo?* A sense of aftershock struck me. I thought I would have great feelings of relief and achievement, but I felt uneasy. Maybe it was seeing Guo's moment of vulnerability, or maybe….

Is it even the right thing to do to let him off the hook with no consequences? Will it really make Guo never do such a thing again, or will the embarrassment do the trick? Even worse, will Guo and Ming insult me more aggressively because they know I would let them get away with it? Perhaps I pretended I had more confidence than I actually have in reality.

People gathered around the game table again once the scroll situation was handled. I managed to put aside my emotions and focus on the game by reanalyzing my cards and making mental notes for each scenario. I had to admit they weren't as bad as I thought initially.

The game resumed. Guo had apparently lost his momentum. It took him a lot longer to put down each card, and he stuttered when he called Pong. I told myself not to

THE UNTOLD TRUTH OF CLUB 門神

be distracted, as the last thing I wanted was to repeat what happened in the last game with Ming.

It was amazing! Not sure what happened but my luck had completely turned around. At each turn, someone put down a card that was exactly what I needed. After picking up a perfect card, I announced "I'm calling."

I heard collective groans and cheers in the crowd. All I needed was either the sixty-thousand card or the blank card. One by one, each player made the call too. At this moment, any of the four of us could win at the next card played.

Hoping either card would magically appear, the images of them repeated in my head each time when I drew a card, or someone's card hit the table until....

Ke shook his head and said, "I know this is a risky card but what else can I do." He put down the sixty-thousand card.

"I won!" I called out, but I wasn't the only one who called it. I looked to the right. Guo needed the same card to win.

There was a brief silence before onlookers looked at each other with their mouths open and started whispering.

"What happens now?" Yao Yao spoke up what was on everyone's tip of tongue, standing next to the white board where she was keeping the scores.

"Guo wins!" Ming yelled and rushed to my side of the table. "Becau...." He glanced at my shelf then stopped abruptly, appearing frustrated. He eyeballed Guo, but Guo kept his head down without a word. I felt vindicated.

My mind flashed back to when Monk Taiyuan was teaching me in a game.

"What if more than one player claims the same card to win?" The five-year-old me asked.

"It doesn't happen too often but when it does, the closest player to the right side of whoever discarded the card wins."

"I'm the closest to Ke's right side," I said confidently, pointing to Ke.

"Cassidy is right," Principal Jiang confirmed. After counting the tokens, he declared, "and...she has the highest score!"

As soon as the realization dawned on everyone, they erupted in cheers! It was so amazingly loud that I couldn't make out any words, just white noises. I stood up in a daze. It was like a dream, like someone scored the last winning point in the national ping pong tournament. There could have been a hundred more people there and I wouldn't know the difference.

"I'm pleased to announce the winner of our first Mahjong tournament. Cassidy Giordano!" Principal Jiang said with a flourish. He congratulated me, shook my hand and laid a medal around my neck.

Loud applause erupted. Among the red sea, Yao Yao was jumping up and down vivaciously. I was speechless and flooded with emotions. After months' preparation and contemplation, I did it. Surrounded by my friends, *I was on top of the world*.

Not long after, it was the countdown to midnight. The sky was on fire. Small flicks of light shot into the air from the courtyard, where many of us made a gigantic circle. The last round of firework was going to go out with a bang, literally. With seconds left, Mr. Peng lit up a pile of the largest firecrackers in the center of the circle.

"…three, two, one!" The whole crowd yelled with excitement. The firecrackers took off, along with the crowds cheering, jumping, and hugging each other.

"HAPPY NEW YEAR!"

CRACK, CRACK, CRACK. Debris scattered in the air, like millions of fireflies taking off into the night sky. Next to my best friends, I cheered with happiness.

I wish this moment never ends.

Someone tapped me on the shoulder. It was Yao Yao. The firecrackers had finally stopped. The air was smokey and smelled like gunpowder.

"Congratulations, Cassidy." She exclaimed, "I'm sooooo glad you won!" Yao Yao's big eyes sparkled.

"Thank you." We exchanged a smirk.

"Hey, Cassidy. Have you heard of Paiya temple?"

"Paiya temple?" I thought I caught the name a few times but knew nothing more.

"Yes, a special temple! Our school sends students to guard it every day, something to do with a portal and birds. Lucky for you because only thirteen-year-olds and above are allowed. I can't wait until I get to guard it!"

Even though it was hard to hear with loud chatters everywhere, we managed to converse. Yao Yao talked in a high pitch with big smiles as she always does, despite it being after midnight. "Have you been there yet?"

"No, I haven't," I smiled back.

"We should go together! How about tomorrow?" Yao Yao's eyes lit up.

"Sure, I'll go."

"Okay, see you then!"

CHAPTER 10:
PAIYA TEMPLE

February 3 (Sunday)

It was Sunday, the New Year's Day. After hours of cleanup of last night's party, it was finally time for me to visit the Paiya temple. Yao Yao and I were supposed to go together, but she canceled at the last minute because she was feeling a bit under the weather. I asked my friends to go along, but they were all busy practicing for a mandatory spell test that was just announced.

Should I go alone? Back when I first arrived, I was warned not to go outside the school gate alone unless in a group of two or more. Ms. Wu told me we're safe inside the fence because it was once blessed by a demigod to keep monsters out. I was a little hesitant because of Mei's experience with Bixi. *But that was at dawn. Today is New Year's Day.* With the sun shining, somehow I felt safe to leave the gate. For one thing, I had nothing else planned. For another, students go there every day so it shouldn't be a big deal.

The forest was overgrown. I hiked up and down the hills along the bumpy path, pushing branches out of the way. At times, I passed some unusually steep slopes that seemed like a large amount of dirt had collapsed. I learned from my geography class that this type of landscape could be caused by floods.

The path eventually opened to an ancient temple, half hidden in the valley. I cautiously approached the gate, which led to the courtyard outlined by two-story buildings. Across from me was the main structure under an arch. It had double roofs, with more pillars and detailed carvings. Gold, red, blue, green, and gold…did I already say gold? In the center of the courtyard was a large round stone well and a bulky water barrel next to it.

I looked around. A few monks were sweeping and organizing things. "Excuse me, what's this temple for?" I asked, taking a half-step over the threshold.

One of the monks stopped sweeping and squinted at me. He didn't seem keen to give information to a stranger. Well, anyone in their right mind shouldn't be, even if that stranger is a thirteen-year-old.

"I'm Cassidy Giordano, from the Paiya Boarding School nearby."

"Oh, I've heard your name," he glared at me and said. "You are not supposed to come here alone. You don't even have a weapon with you."

"My friend Yao Yao was supposed to come with me, but she feels sick," I said hesitantly. *Am I going to be in trouble?*

"Since this is your first violation, you get a warning. I'll have to report to your principal if it happens again. Do you understand?"

"Yes, I promise." I nodded.

"Good. You need to walk back with the two students when they're done."

I nodded again.

The monk finally broke out a little smile and asked, "What do you want to know?"

"What's this temple for?"

"Well, this is Paiya temple. Your school sends two shifts of two Menshens to guard this door every day." The monk turned around and pointed to a half-moon shaped door on the main structure. "Inside this door is a portal to heaven. It allows the magpies to fly freely between heaven and earth."

My jaw dropped and froze.

"On the night of July 7th every year, all Menshens from your school come to guard the door. This is the night most magpies fly to heaven and back."

Something clicked in my head. Two pieces of this story sounded familiar. July 7th...magpies.... It was a lot like the widely known legend I grew up with!

The legend says the seventh daughter of the Jade Emperor once came down to Earth and fell in love with a young cowherd named Niulang. She wanted to stay with him forever, but the emperor demanded his daughter come back. Niulang was heartbroken and chased after her who was taken by the emperor guards. Before he could catch up with them, the Queen Mother of the West took off her hairpin and drew a river in front of Niulang so he couldn't cross. This is the Milky Way (银河系). Eventually, the Jade Emperor was touched by their love. He allowed them to meet on a bridge made of Magpies over the Milky Way, but only once a year on the night of July 7th.

I grew up knowing this legend for as long as I could remember. I was fascinated, thinking it was a fantasy my entire life then finding out it was real! I couldn't help but wonder how many other legends were real as well. I stood there staring at the door, imagining a flock of beautiful black and white magpies coming and leaving.

"Why does this door need to be guarded?"

"Monsters," The monk continued, "who are enemies of the Jade Emperor. They want to anger him by killing the birds that make up the bridge. The job of protecting this door is given to Menshens."

I thought maybe magpies tasted delicious, but this made more sense. Out of nowhere, some noises emerged from the main building.

"Can I go inside?" I asked.

"You may." The monk said and resumed sweeping.

I approached the door and slowly pushed it open with excitement. *What does a portal to heaven look like?*

The ceiling was tall and pointy with a circular opening in the middle. In the center of the floor was a column of misty air mass, circulating continuously in a spiral toward the top and then dissipating through the opening. The air felt cool and incredibly refreshing.

Two girls stood next to it, both holding a spear in one hand. They didn't seem surprised as they must have heard me outside.

"Hi, Cassidy!" One of the girls greeted me eagerly, squinting her eyes behind thick glasses. Her long black hair almost reached her waist. She looked familiar to me. "Congrats on winning the Mahjong tournament! My friend Lu told me about you. I'm Pingye Yu."

"Oh, hi! I saw you singing with Lu at the top of your lungs last night."

Pingye chuckled and pointed to the other girl. "This is Li'an Yang. We're two grades above you."

Li'an was tall and slender with pale skin, wearing a white fuzzy shirt, kind of like a puffy cloud. She had a white belt that held a piece of bamboo with randomly shaped carvings on the exterior. It looked like a flute. *Maybe she was blessed by the music god, if there is one.*

Li'an stared at me with a muddled look. "Um...hi, Cassidy, so you're not from China?"

"Li'an, don't be rude!" Pingye quickly interrupted.

"It's fine. I'm Italian." I was used to this kind of question growing up in China.

"That's nice, Cassidy," Li'an said in a quiet tone. Two dimples formed on her cheeks as she gave a half-hearted smile, although her eyes didn't tell the same story.

Li'an opened a bit after noticing I was staring at her flute. "Oh, this is my flute." She stepped outside and brought the flute to her lips. Instead of hearing what a normal flute would play, it sounded like a slow melody with a sizzling sound. Nonetheless, it was calming.

Still playing, Li'an stared into the far distance like she was searching for something. She stopped, then an echo emerged. Li'an listened attentively until the echo diminished, as if it was anticipated and meant something to her. Maybe it was just me, but somehow, I sensed an aura of sadness around Li'an. It was hard to explain. I'd say she was courteous but faintly aloof.

I was intrigued by the flute. Li'an saw my expression and handed the flute to me carefully. Having never played one before, it sounded like...how do I describe? High-pitched

THE UNTOLD TRUTH OF CLUB 門神

whistles from a boiling teapot. No echo either. *Maybe Li'an has a special way of playing it.*

"It sounded just like that when I played it too." Pingye laughed. "Do you know I was blessed by the god of hearing, Shunfeng'er?"

"Wow... How far can you hear?" I asked.

"I can hear living things and objects a hundred meters away," Pingye said proudly. "Most of the time, I'm able to filter out the background noises."

So Pingye must have had her One Chance already. I think it's interesting that Pingye wore glasses, like it leveled out her advanced hearing capabilities.

"But I'm as blind as a bat without my glasses." Pingye giggled. Suddenly, she paused. "I heard a thud."

"I didn't hear anything. Where was it?" I asked, scanning around.

"The dungeon I think," Pingye said without any worry in her voice. "You know this temple has a dungeon, right?"

NOW THERE'S A DUNGEON. This place has everything, doesn't it?

"No, no, I didn't," I said a lot more calmly than how I felt. *I mean who knows what's down there!*

As I was imagining all the terrifying monsters or humans that wouldn't hesitate a second to kill me, Pingye suggested, "I need to check it. Do you want to come with me?"

I choked in response.

"You'll be fine. Most likely something fell," Pingye reassured me.

"I'll stay here." Lia'an encouraged me. "Pingye can take you. She'll hear if anything is coming well before I see it."

"Great. I'm getting a little bored anyway." Pingye let out a laugh. "Come on, Cassidy. You should get used to this sort of thing!"

Before my brain had a chance to render what was happening, Pingye grabbed my hand and took me to the other side of the courtyard. I couldn't help but notice the strange looks from the monks, probably processing the sight of a child dragging another terrified child. Usually I'm curious, but wanting to visit where dangerous beasts are kept is a whole different level of curiosity!

We stopped at a smaller building with slanted red roofs pointing up and balconies held by red pillars. Pingye opened the squeaky door. In front of me was a table draped with red cloth. On top of it were small gold statues and so many candles that they must be a fire hazard. As soon as I saw creepy looking stone stairs in the back leading to the basement, my breathing stopped for a few seconds.

"What's exactly kept down there?" I asked while being led down the stairs. After I got over the initial shock, my curiosity got the best of me.

"Menshens who turned on us, or monsters captured by us and can be used for our benefit." Pingye turned to me and paused her steps. "Have you heard of the legend of One-Armer yet?"

"Yeah. It's Hao, right?"

"Well, Hao stole some rare books from the Underground Library. The legend says she was kept in the dungeon after they caught her."

"What happened to Hao in the end?" I asked curiously.

"She died young, in her cell."

"Oh!" I was taken back.

"Don't worry. It's usually empty for as long as I remember." Pingye comforted me after noticing my reaction. Just when I was about to sigh with relief, Pingye added, "But again, I don't keep up with what they put in here. So, we could have a surprise!"

We reached the bottom. It was windowless with dim lighting. In front of us was a narrow stone walkway stretching fifteen meters to the left and right. Unoccupied cells lined up on both sides. Above us were arches every two meters supporting the low ceiling.

"Pingye, what's that?" I pointed to a faint but visible line along the wall.

"The water stains? I heard this dungeon was once filled with water from a serious flood. The good thing is they built a drainage system, so it hasn't flooded since." Pingye tapped a drainage pipe with her foot.

The dungeon didn't seem too awful. Sure, it was dark and creepy, but Pingye strolled along like she was in a field of dandelions and everything was fine. So, I guess it was. We reached the end of one side, where the cells ended.

"It doesn't look like anything is kept here right now," Pingye said in a disappointed tone.

"I'd hope not."

"Well, I can still show you the other side."

"What else is there to see?"

"Who knows? But I'd rather not stand in the same spot for another hour."

"I see, so you'd rather stay inside a creepy dungeon than stand next to a portal to heaven?" I said jokingly.

"Exactly." We both laughed.

We reached the last cell on the other side. Pingye said it was where Hao was kept, according to rumors. Then something long and off-white caught my eye.

"That must be the pipe that made the noise," Pinye said, pointing to the rusty white pipe that laid on the floor inside. "Sometimes they fall from the ceiling since they're too old." She unlatched the door and picked up the pipe.

I followed Pingye closely. "I guess we're don..." I stopped cold. Something emerged from the darkness in the corner of the cell.

A *beast*. On its front were rough scales as black as the darkest night, while its belly was covered with soft white fur. The beast was ready to pounce at us.

"Cassidy, leave!" Pingye shouted as I sprinted out of the cell.

Pingye quickly slammed the door behind her, but the door was jammed before it could be fully latched. The beast threw itself onto the door, determined to destroy the only thing that stood in its way. *BANG, BANG, BANG*. It crashed its head again and again on the door, making loud rattling sounds. Pure terror was coursing through me. *What if it gets out?*

"Go outside! I can't fight in a narrow space!" Pingye yelled. We sprinted as fast as we could.

Then I heard a loud clang. The beast broke free. It began to approach us and roared in a strange sound, like a mix of tiger roars and a bird chirping.

"I shouldn't have brought you here!" Pingye shouted, breathing heavily while running.

"I know!"

THE UNTOLD TRUTH OF CLUB 門神

Reaching the top of the stairs, I looked behind. My eyes *met* the furious eyes of a monster. Chills ran through my spine. It was merely steps away from me. We barely made it out of the building, and out of breath at the same time.

"Wha..." Li'an trailed off, noticing the urgency of the situation.

"There's a monster loose!" Pingye yelled, "Cassidy, run!"

As if on cue, the beast appeared from behind the door, and roared its strange sound again.

I bolted out of the gate and into the forest. Grabbing on a large tree branch, I climbed up and peeked through the leaves. My heart was pounding fast. Through a small opening, I watched the monster fight for the first time in my life.

Pingye, Li'an and monks swiftly moved around in a circle homing in on the roaring beast. Their Kung Fu skills were flawless. Spinning, jumping, punching, kicking, and stabbing...all in graceful but powerful movements as if their bodies were weightless. The monster swung its paw in all directions, while dodging the spears and arrows using the water barrel as a shield. Whenever the beast tried to back out, there was always someone behind him, twisting and turning their spears.

Hiding in the safety net of a tree, a surge of guilt ran through me. Something was telling me to help, but I didn't move. *I'll be killed if I try.*

The beast slashed its paw toward a monk, but suddenly changed direction to Pingye. She fell backwards, wincing. To my surprise, Pingye bounced up in an instant, and jabbed the spear straight to its heart. The monster collapsed in a flash. It dropped dead.

I sighed in relief and dashed back to the temple, passing some monks who were removing the body of the monster. Both Pingye and Li'an looked exhausted. Pingye sat on the floor, blood dripping from an open cut on her chin.

Li'an scooped out a first aid kit from a storage chest. She cleaned the wound and said to Ping'ye calmly, "Now stay still." Li'an extended her hand forward and her eyes were fixed on the wound without blinking. Unbelievably, the tip of the cut began to slowly close while Li'an's arm was slightly shaking in the process. When the cut was about halfway through healing, Li'an dropped her arm, looking exhausted.

"That's incredible!" I exclaimed, amazed by her healing power.

Li'an smiled and brought her arm up again for round two.

"Thanks, Li'an!" Pingye stopped her. "Save your energy. I'm fine with just some gauze." She reached over to the first-aid kit.

"It was extremely brave of you. What kind of monster was it?" I waited until Li'an finished with the patch.

"I'm not sure. It's new to me," said Li'an.

"Me either," Pingye said while looking out, "Well, it's seven o'clock. The next two students just got here. We should get going. I need to stop by the school clinic."

Later in the evening, I was resting on my bed writing my diary. I thought I heard a vague sound, something like a...cat.

THE UNTOLD TRUTH OF CLUB 門神

How to describe the sound? Well, I don't know exactly, like it was in danger and meowed...urgently? It kept going on and getting louder. I decided to find out what it was.

Once outside, the sound became much clearer. I'm pretty sure the entire dorm heard it. I figured the sound came from behind the building, so I walked toward the back.

"Do you hear that noise?" I asked two shadows walking by. I didn't really know them but I think they're a couple grades above me.

"Noise? Or the wind?" They looked at me as if I said I saw a flying monkey. They continued their way.

I stopped at the back of the building. There was the water tower. The concrete floor was damp with no direct light. No cat, but I could still hear the meowing louder than ever. I even inspected the sewer drain to make sure no cat was trapped down there.

Out of nowhere, I heard something dashing in the crisp air toward me. I turned and saw a shining golden ring the size of a scallion pancake, spinning and heading straight to me! I ducked on instinct, covering my head with both hands. After a few seconds, I peeked. The golden ring was one meter away paused in mid-air, like it was inspecting me. Then it turned around and flew away as fast as it came. The meow sound ceased as soon as the ring disappeared out of my view.

I was left shocked, staring at the path where the golden ring used to be. It was so out of place. *Is it dog mythology now?* Since any dog would love an autonomous fetch toy.

If you're confused, actually you must be confused, you're not alone because I had no clue what just happened. I wasn't even sure if I should tell someone or if anyone would believe me. They'd think I was crazy because I appeared to be the only person who heard the meow that led me to the ring. The two boys seemed to be unaware of it while they should be.

Nevertheless, the ring seemed harmless...for the moment. *I'll search for golden rings in Chinese mythology when the computer isn't occupied.*

CHAPTER 11:
A FIGURE IN THE RAIN
February 3 (Sunday 10 pm)

I thought nothing else would happen for the rest of the night, but I was wrong.

I barely fell asleep when I heard a loud thud downstairs. Minutes later, running footsteps were pounding on the floor below me, with an eruption of worried voices.

"What happened?"

"Is she okay?"

I jumped out of my bed. Obviously, I wasn't the only one who heard it. A few students rushed downstairs along with me.

A crowd of students already stood there in a circle. In the center were a few school medics on their knees attending someone on the floor. One of them signaled the crowd to quiet down.

It's Pingye! She appeared to be motionless and...lifeless. *What happened to her? She was fine just hours ago!* A lump formed in my throat. Everyone watched on while the medics transferred Pingye to a stretcher and carried her away.

I spotted Lingling in the crowd. "Lingling, what happened?" I was almost afraid of hearing the answer.

Lingling turned around with the look of a full-on panic attack. Her breath was short and quick. I had never seen her like that. Tears kept running down Lingling's face, which she didn't even bother to wipe away. Lingling glanced at me and sped away.

"Lingling?" I was frightened, not just for Pingye but for Lingling as well.

"Not now." Lingling continued walking, her voice shaking.

The crowd of students had slowly dispersed one by one. By this time, only one other person was still here. It was Lu.

Lu slumped against the wall, stone-faced with wet eyes. He stared at the floor blankly, like a completely different person from who he was yesterday.

"Lu, are you okay? What happened to Pingye?"

"I don't know." Lu sounded deeply distressed, avoiding eye contact with me. Which question he was answering, I wasn't sure.

The air was heavy. The night was dreadful. Lu eventually got up and departed without another word.

BEEP, BEEP, BEEP. A loud siren suddenly went off, breaking the deadly silence. *What now?*

"Everyone, please stay inside," A loudspeaker repeated. "This is a flash flood warning."

Soon after, a flare of lightning zipped across the dark sky and lit it up like fireworks. Seconds later, BOOM! Crashing thunder roared fiercely, making my heart leap out of my chest. Before I knew it, another electrifying giant

THE UNTOLD TRUTH OF CLUB 門神

spark flashed in the sky, followed by an even louder BOOM and BANG! I covered both of my ears.

In the blink of an eye, a downpour was pounding on the ground. Large raindrops hit the windows, fast and furious. *Is the night ever going to end?*

Looking out the window, a dark figure was dashing to the field holding something tight. I squinted. *Who'd be out now?*

Another lightning bolt flashed in the distance, revealing the figure...*Lingling*. She held a pot similar to the one I saw before, running under the pouring rain as if her life depended on it. I had a pretty good guess as to where she was heading. *The pond*. I saw her there a few times with her pot, but why now? Her panicked face minutes ago flashed before my eyes.

Does she know about the flood warning? She can't be out there. It's dangerous!

I ran to my room to grab a flashlight. Mei was still sleeping, even the lightning and thunder didn't wake her up. I flew down the stairs, while the alarm was still screeching in my ears. I jerked the door open. Suddenly, a gust of cold air and water invited itself in. I pointed my flashlight to the haze. *No one.*

I knew it was just a warning. The flash flood may happen any minute or not at all. Nonetheless, I bolted out. The heavy raindrops drenched me immediately. I headed straight to the pond in the woods even though it was obviously a bad idea with the lightning.

I maneuvered through the trees, jumping over puddles and roots, ducking under branches. "LINGLING!" I shouted, scanning the woods. No response. I shouted again and again.

BANG! Lightning danced in the sky once more. I looked up through the branches and leaves, as fear trembled through me.

There's no monster here. Nothing can break in. The gate's there and secure. I thought over and over again to reassure myself.

I slowed down when the woods parted. The once peaceful pond gleamed with thousands of ripples revealed by my flashlight. Lingling was nowhere in sight. Meanwhile, I was soaking wet, catching up with my breath. I groaned, *where is she?*

I stood under the cover of a tree to hide from the raindrops that felt like needles. *Lingling wouldn't stay here for long. Maybe she's already back in her room.* With one last glance at the pond, I turned around.

Soon, the soft glow of the dorm buildings came into view, along with the distant sound of the alarm. Shivering from the cold, I ran across the field to get back inside. Once the door was shut behind me, the sound of the rain was muffled but quickly replaced by the loud BEEP BEEP BEEP. I sighed, glad that it was at least dry here.

Carrying my soaked shoes, I sprinted up the stairs leaving wet footprints behind. I knocked on her door anxiously. *Please be in your room, Lingling.*

The doorknob turned and opened up halfway. "Lingling?" I asked.

"Cassidy?" Lingling stood there half hidden behind the door. She was *dripping wet* with her hair down, out of its usual bun.

THE UNTOLD TRUTH OF CLUB 門神

I sighed. "Thank goodness you're safe. I saw you running outside and was looking for you."

Lingling looked away and murmured, "Oh. I just forgot something. I'm fine."

"So did you find it?"

"Yeah," Lingling avoided looking at me and said in a small voice.

"Okay. I'll go now. Good night." I wasn't in a mood to inquire any further at this point.

"Good night." Lingling added hesitantly, "Thank you for looking for me...I mean it."

Back in my room, my head was still spinning over everything. *What happened to Pingye? What's so important that Lingling had to run in the storm? Why did she bring the pot with her? Is she lying?*

I think it'll be a little harder to fall asleep tonight.

CHAPTER 12:
DISEASE DISASTER

February 4 (Monday 7 am)

The howling wind almost knocked me off my feet on my way to the morning class. There was a small flood later last night. Since I couldn't sleep, I spent hours looking out the window watching the water rush by. This morning, the water had retreated but the ground was still soaking wet. Some trees were knocked down. Inside the vegetable garden, all the crops were ripped from the ground, and the soil became a swamp of mud.

My mind was still fully occupied by Pingye.

I entered the classroom where students gathered in circles chatting intensely. No teacher. Of course, the news of Pingye had spread overnight. Ten minutes later, still no teacher and the classroom was getting louder. The room was full of theories, and whether the late teacher had anything to do with Pingye. It was probably twenty minutes in when we finally decided to send someone to inquire with Principal Jiang.

Running and out of breath, Mr. Peng finally turned up. He took a moment to catch his breath. "We have to gather in the cafeteria. Come quickly," He said in an urgent tone.

Everyone got up, whispering while heading to the cafe. A bunch of other classes beat us to it. A few teachers were telling students to stay back, and Principal Jiang would explain to us in a second. Today seemed to be filled with endless waiting.

Finally, Principal Jiang stepped up to the front, with a serious look on his face. Ms. Wu stood beside him, nervously straightening her black jacket.

"Everybody, please listen carefully," Principal Jiang stated. The chatter died down instantly. "One of our pupils, Pingye Yu, fell into a serious coma."

I blinked away my tears.

"It's a mythical illness, so we can't send her to the hospital," Principal Jiang continued in a gloomy tone. "We aren't certain how to treat her either."

"How bad is it?" One of the students piped up. Neither Principal Jiang or Ms. Wu responded, which led to more serious concerns.

"Wait, how bad?" I said in worry, to no one in particular.

"A dangerous coma with no cure?" Another classmate added, "Deadly bad."

Suddenly, the image of Lingling running in the rain from last night flashed before my eyes. *Does she know something?* I looked at Lingling in real time. She was biting her lips and seemed to be spaced out. I brushed my thoughts aside to focus on listening.

"However," Ms. Wu spoke softly, "we're able to put together a list of ingredients based on Chinese traditional medicine to treat coma. In addition, we identified a few very rare items." Ms. Wu gave us some hope at least.

Have you seen in cartoons when people open a list and it's like a mile long? Well, this was as close as it could get. Ms. Wu started to unfold a long piece of paper with endless ingredients.

"I need four groups of four to five students to find all the ingredients as soon as possible," Ms. Wu said hastily. "Form groups as you wish and write your names on a piece of paper. Four groups will be picked by raffle. Lastly, only students thirteen and above are allowed."

"We should put our names in," Lu said immediately in a determined voice.

"Definitely," Lingling added without any hesitation.

"I'll go if you guys want to go too." Bo turned to look at Mei and myself who hadn't said anything.

"Absolutely," Mei responded.

I opened my mouth, but no words came out. *I want to save Pingye so badly, but the truth is I won't be of much help. Wouldn't I just be dead weight? Can I even fight under pressure? Sure, I took classes, but it wasn't a life-or-death situation. I haven't even mastered the fire spell yet.*

My friends were staring at me as if asking *please come with us*. Only a few seconds to decide. *The pros. I'll have a chance to save Pingye, and that's the biggest pro. I don't want to disappoint my friends either. The serious con is I'm not nearly as good as Menshens. So if I ever die on a trip, it'll probably be this one.*

"I'll go," I blurted out, surprising myself. After all, there was a good chance we wouldn't be picked anyway.

Soon many volunteer groups put their pieces of paper in a basket. Ms. Wu started picking from the basket randomly and handed them to Principal Jiang.

THE UNTOLD TRUTH OF CLUB 門神

"First group. Ke Zhang, Xiao Zou, Yong Hua, Li'an Yang." Principal Jiang read out loud. I quickly glanced at Li'an. She was looking at Principal Jiang with a proud smile on her face.

"Second group. Lu Sun, Lingling Sun, Bo Chen, Mei Cao, Cassidy Giordano." *What? Is it real or am I dreaming?* While he was going down the list, I was in complete disbelief that our group got picked from probably twenty-five other groups!

Minutes later, Mei tugged on my arm while I was still comprehending what had happened, "Cassidy, Cassidy! Come on! We need to go pick our weapons!"

"Pick our weapons?" I looked over and noticed some people were following Principal Jiang.

"Yeah, we're not going empty-handed."

All the chosen groups were led into a room that we had to squeeze to fit. The walls were lined with weapons, like swords, spears, axes, bows and arrows. Principal Jiang stood behind a short table, as if behind a cash register, asking which one we would like.

"Choose your weapons. Spear or bow and arrow. Please remember axes and swords are only for fifteen and up," Principal Jiang said while pointing to a blue sign on the table SWORDS AND AXES: FIFTEEN AND UP.

Everyone rushed to choose a weapon like they would run out. Most of them grabbed spears. I glanced at the wall. All the weapons looked freshly sharpened but used, with scratches and some dented edges.

I grabbed a spear. It was an easy decision for me. I barely held a bow and arrow in my life. The only time when I was practicing my stance, I released the bow without an arrow, and the string ended up snapping in half!

Mei and Bo chose the spear as well. Lu held a bow and arrow, but Lingling only took arrows, no bow.

"Don't you need a bow?" I asked curiously.

"No, I use water," Lingling said as if it explained everything.

I heard she had some kind of power over water, but I couldn't figure out how it applies to bow and arrows.

"The water wraps around arrows like this." Lingling opened one of her water bottles, poured some water out, and guided it to form a thin layer of water around the arrow. When I say guided, I mean she used telekinetics to move the water around the arrow. It looked so mesmerizing. If I were her, I could play with it all day.

"I'm able to control which way the arrow goes. Lu can do it as well." Lingling said.

"But I can only control a third of the water needed to make it work, so I have to use a bow," Lu added.

"Wow! I guess you were both blessed by the water god then?" I asked as Lingling guided the water back into the bottle.

"I don't know." Lu cleared his throat loudly while pushing up his glasses. "I don't know."

"Hebo," Lingling inserted abruptly, "god of rivers."

Lu walked out of the room.

There's something odd going on with the twins.

It was our turn to find out what ingredients we needed to obtain. Principal Jiang instructed our group to obtain two rare items, rather than a bunch of small items like the other groups got.

"First, you must collect a dragon scale." Principal Jiang started. "It's dangerous and nearly impossible to remove the scale fresh off the dragon. Make sure to use your weapon and be cautious. This dragon lives on the border of Wufeng Mountain. Secondly, you need to obtain the lotus flower seeds in Nasha Wetlands, where the god Goumang had recently relocated the kingdom. It is rumored that Goumang has blessed a particular lotus flower with healing power.

"There is a boat owned by our school for decades. It was once blessed by a demigod and became enchanted with speed ever since. It's yours to use but make sure to take good care of it. Come back as soon as possible. We don't know how much time we have to save Pingye before it's too late."

"Cassidy." Ms. Wu pulled me aside and looked straight into my eyes. "Frankly, you should have an idea of what you're getting into. I understand if you want to pull out. You're new, and the mission is risky."

"Thank you, but I *do* want to go." *Too late to back out now.*

"Okay then." Ms. Wu was dead serious. "But I must tell you the most important rule is to listen to the Menshens. They've been trained and know what to do in quests like this. Don't forget to carry your weapon and backpack at all times. You never know when a monster may strike, or situations may arise."

Ms. Wu continued on things like preparing for the unexpected, staying alert of the surroundings, not touching things that look suspicious, and how to ask for help if the situation becomes too dangerous. I listened closely.

"Please remember what I said. I want to see you back alive." Ms. Wu looked at me for confirmation.

A vague image popped into my head. I was inside a car, and a voice said, "I'll be right back, Cassidy. Don't go anywhere."

Hours passed, day turned to night, and there was still no one coming back.

I shook off the thoughts and nodded to Ms. Wu. Each of us got supplies. After we grabbed personal items from our rooms, the five of us regrouped at the doorway. We agreed on our itinerary, which was to search for the dragon scale first then go to Nasha wetland.

Another group walked by us, led by Li'an. "Did I hear someone say Nasha wetland?" Li'an paused to ask.

"Yes, we need lotus flower seeds from there." Lu was quick to answer.

"Alright." Li'an smiled at us while carefully adjusting the flute on her belt. "Best of luck." She waved at us before walking out of the dorm with her group.

Just before we headed out, Lingling opened her backpack to check for something. I caught a glimpse of her clothes all packed in perfect squares. I just shoved mine in. *Wait!* There was something else. In the corner of her backpack was the distinctive blue-striped pot shaped like a squeezed pumpkin. It looked like the same pot she was holding last night in the thunderstorm. *Why does she always carry the pot?*

Li'an's group disappeared into the distance. Recalling the golden plaques on the wall, I asked, "Is the trip going to be dangerous?"

THE UNTOLD TRUTH OF CLUB 門神

"Yes," All of them said in unison. I don't know why I even asked. There was no way their answers would be any different.

"There has never been a trip when it was easy, *ever*," Bo told me, which did not help.

"You should be fine as long as you're with us." Mei noticed my nervousness.

"Should" be fine, but not *"will" be fine.*

"Ms. Wu gave you instructions, right?" Lingling added, "The best thing you can do is to make sure you follow her advice exactly."

On our way to the boat, I kept wondering if I made the right choice. *On the one hand, I think it's incredible what Menshens are willing to do for each other. Almost a third of the school volunteered to put their lives on the line to save Pingye. I'm proud of becoming part of it.*

On the other hand, do I really know how dangerous of a job it is to be on a mission? If I do, why did I sign up? Dozens of others can do this better than me, so wouldn't it be better to have a Menshen take my place? It was peer pressure.

Overall, I wasn't sure how to make out of the whole Menshen thing...kind of like a mixed feeling of excitement and fear, but mostly fear. Something told me this trip won't be easy.

CHAPTER 13:
THE ROGUE WAVE
February 5 (Monday 8 am)

Looking out to the east, the sky was filled with layers of long stretches of clouds, where sun rays illuminated in various shades of red, pink, orange, and yellow. It was breathtakingly beautiful. Have you heard of *"Red at night, sailor's delight; Red in the morning, sailor's warning?"* Well, it wasn't like we had a choice on when to leave. Pingyc nccded help urgently.

It took us thirty minutes to go down the mountain and locate the boat at the shore. Lu pulled off the white cover, revealing an ordinary-looking boat shaped like a canoe. It was made of dark wood with a faint white stripe along the side. The boat had a flat canvas top, which I imagine would be very helpful when traveling. A map was laying on the front seat. Lu grabbed it immediately.

We pushed the boat to the water and settled down. To my delight, the boat gave a great jolt and sped off at full throttle in the blink of an eye. Everyone else cheered with excitement. *Do people cheer when they're heading to their doom?*

"Lu, how far is Wufeng Mountain from here?" I yelled over the sound of water breaking.

Lu opened the map. It took him unexpectedly long to figure it out. "Well," he scratched his head and said, "based on the map, it's like twelve hours!"

"How do you know that?" Lingling was skeptical. "It only gives you the distance, not hours."

"Someone hand-wrote the speed of this boat on the map." Lu was about to throw the map to Lingling when she quickly grabbed it before the wind blew it away. "Divide the distance by speed, and you get twelve hours. That's not even including the bathroom breaks! If you don't believe me, check the math yourself."

Lingling examined it then announced, "You're right."

"Told you so." Lu looked away.

Everything went smoothly at first, except occasionally when someone moved to the front and stood up (cough-cough-Mei), the boat would get flipped over. Nothing got damaged though. It went like this. Someone stood up, then we immediately told that person to sit down. She said it's going to be fine, right before all of us fell into the cold water. Thankfully the boat stopped for us. Imagine the same thing happening three times! Luckily, we were able to get back onto the boat, except we had to pull Bo up since he couldn't swim.

Remember I said it was a windy day? Well, we were going fast especially with the wind pushing us, but a storm started to brew hours later.

It began pouring. I usually don't get severe motion sickness, but that started to change. The boat rocked back and forth rapidly with strong waves, enough to make everyone nauseous. Mei was the only one who seemed okay and she was even READING, which would make it a hundred times worse. I scooched to the stern to throw up. We had made an unspoken rule that whenever you need to do that, you go to the stern.

The sun was diminishing. Mei read the manual while shining a flashlight on it. Someone was smart enough to cover it in plastic. Mei yelled something about what to do if we got stuck in a serious storm. "Listen! We must call on a sea goddess, Tianhou (天后), to give us guidance, but you should ca…"

I didn't hear Mei finish her sentence because Lu cut her off. "Goddess Tianhou! Help us!" Lu yelled, leaning over the boat.

"Lu!" Mei screamed over the sound of roaring waves.

"What? What did I do wrong?" Lu asked with wide eyes.

"You're not supposed to call her by *that* name!"

"Why?" Lu was coughing and obviously confused.

"That's her formal name. Now we'll have to wait longer for her to come!"

Bo turned his head, as if he already knew the reason.

"I'll explain, Bo," Mei said loudly, noticing that Bo just became occupied with another situation. "You're supposed to call her by her casual name, Mazu (妈祖), so she'll come quicker. If you call her formal name, she'll take longer to prepare herself. You, Lu, called her Tianhou, her formal name!"

Guessing from Mei's tone, I imagined she would have been glaring at Lu. I felt the same way. We desperately needed help. If Lu waited one more second, he would've known what to say. It could make a difference in life or death!

THE UNTOLD TRUTH OF CLUB 門神

"Is it too late to call her casual name now?" Lu was holding on to a thread of hope.

"Yes." Mei was crushed. "Tianhou is mute. I have no idea how she is going to give advice either."

The storm only got worse after that.

The sky was draped in dark gray clouds. The rain was pouring down fast and furious as if the sky had opened a giant leak hole. The wind screamed in my ears. The waves crashing against the boat while sweeping over was overwhelming.

Sea water was slowly rising inside the boat. Fortunately, I didn't think the water weight would make the boat sink or slow it down, because we were still going as fast as before. However, there were numerous times when I thought the boat was about to flip over for sure. I was soaked in salty water, praying the goddess would arrive soon and give us godly advice.

"When will the goddess come?" I shouted at Mei over the pounding waves.

"The manual didn't say!"

I was nervous about the odds of us dying. I felt too weak and sick to do anything, but I worried all it took was one strong wave to overturn our boat and we would be sucked under the water.

Ironically, that was exactly what was going to happen next. Minutes later, an enormous wave shaped like a steep white wall was crashing toward us fiercely. It seemed small in the distance but was probably three times taller than us and it kept growing taller. My head started spinning relentlessly with many scenarios. Well, it was only one scenario-*the giant wave sweeping over us.*

I couldn't even begin to think how worried Bo must have been. Actually, I wasn't sure how much of a difference swimming skills would make in this dire situation anyway. The water force was too strong. The boat was also very questionable. *Will it stay in shape, be torn from impact, or get carried away by the waves?*

While those thoughts flashed through my head, something in front of us started to shimmer and grew bigger until it became a ball of bright light. I didn't know why but the light made me feel reassured somehow. Even better, the light materialized into what looked like a woman, who was wearing a red dress and a flat-top imperial cap on her head. She took out a whiteboard and a marker.

Is this Tianhou? It doesn't make sense because Tianhou is at least a thousand years old. But who knows? She may have adapted to modern times.

I waited anxiously for the goddess's advice. Tianhou started to write on the whiteboard. This was one of those times I wish everyone would write in English because it took so long to write in Chinese! After what felt like forever, Tianhou turned the board to face us.

This was what she wrote-跳入水中;你會安全的. It means *Jump into the water; You will be safe.*

WHAT? Jump into the water? The wave was looking bigger than ever! I started to question whether this was the right goddess, or a demon trying to get a good laugh at our expense.

"ARE YOU CRAZY!" Lu exclaimed over the wind.

Tianhou smiled calmly and changed the words on the board to *"everyone is"*. *WHAT DOES THAT EVEN MEAN?*

Lu looked down at the water like a dangerous beast was about to swallow him, and he had to jump right into its mouth.

"I can't believe I'm doing this!" I caught Lu shouting desperately before he jumped in. I thought the strong current would sweep him away instantly. Surprisingly, Lu stayed in the same spot in the water without moving, as if the current was non-existent. He looked up and gestured for us to come.

Lingling followed, so did Mei.

Looking at the incoming giant wave then at Bo, something told me Bo wouldn't have the courage to jump in on his own. I know I wouldn't if I couldn't swim. The wave was getting bigger and closer than ever. Without any other options, I grabbed Bo's wrist and counted loudly, *three, two, one*. Bo quickly caught on what to do and jumped in with me.

I crashed into the water with Bo. It was surprising to feel...how to describe this, airy? Not dry. My body was completely wet, but I found myself in a warm cube of air in the water with everyone else. If you're confused, imagine it's a fish tank but the glass isn't there. Inside the air cube, it was easy to stay afloat, keep my head above the water and do nothing.

"I guess everyone is crazy," Lingling said with a bit of a grin.

CRASH! It sounded like rolling thunder. The giant wave had made such an impact that I was afraid our pocket of air would cave in. In a few seconds, the wave rolled over us entirely then continued forward.

The wave finally passed us. All five of us were floating in the water untouched. By this time, Tianhou had disappeared. I looked around and something caught my eyes.

"Is that our boat?" I said, not daring to believe it.

"But it's impossible!" Mei exclaimed.

"I don't know, and I don't care. We still have a boat!" Lu said happily. It seemed unrealistic that our boat would have stayed here. Maybe it popped up after the wave passed, or it could be because of Tianhou. After all, I had no problem believing a thousand-year-old goddess carrying a whiteboard and marker around.

All of us grabbed the rope that was attached to the boat, which prevented us from being carried away by the current.

After the storm completely passed, peace had returned. We climbed onto the boat covered in seaweed, some shells and a (hopefully dead) fish. We continued our course to Wufeng Mountain. I sat in the boat, still in aftershock. I remembered reading about a type of giant wave named "rogue wave". I learned that rogue waves are very rare but extremely dangerous. There's no fighting chance we would still be alive if not for Tianhou.

Hours later, I woke up from a nap and saw land. I yawned. "Lu, you have the map. Is this our first stop?"

"No," Lu said, "we enter this river and follow it for almost one more hour."

Weaving through villages, there were a few dams along the way. We got off the boat, walked on the riverbank and pulled the boat until we passed the dam. It slowed us down in addition to traveling against the current.

It was 11:30 pm when we landed. Under the moonlight was the silhouette of huge mountains. It was probably a giant majestic green mountain, or you could simply say it's a mountain covered with leaves instead of bare rocks.

THE UNTOLD TRUTH OF CLUB 門神

"How do we even know where to go?" I broke the silence after hiking for a while in the leafy mountain.

"Well, from what I remember, a dragon lives here," Lu said, not answering my question.

"What's that noise?" Bo gasped, turning his head around.

A faint sound of bashing rocks emerged from the distance, getting closer and closer.

"Strange. Am I hallucinating?" asked Lu.

"You can't be hallucinating if other people hear it too, dummy." That was Lingling speaking.

A yellow-red leopard-like creature appeared from darkness. It had black spots, five long tails, deadly sharp claws, and an enormous horn right on its forehead. In case you're wondering, it looked nothing like a unicorn. I was speechless. My hands were starting to quiver. My heart was thumping rapidly.

"Stay calm," Lingling whispered. "Now back up *slowly*. Stay behind the trees. I think it's Zheng."

Zheng didn't seem to notice us, yet. We scrambled to hide behind a thick tree. With shaking hands, I grabbed the spear from my back as quietly as I could.

"We can either outrun it, stay put, or fight. Zheng doesn't know we're here." Lu sounded rational at first but suddenly changed his tone. "Wait. What is it doing now?"

Zheng was moving its tail in weird movements. I didn't even notice it was coming closer until it reached within ten steps. Suddenly, it growled at us belligerently.

Without a word, all of us sprinted as fast as we could. I kept running and eventually my feet started to feel weightless. I wouldn't say we have a good head start, but we were able to outrun it, *barely.*

In a wild forest, there isn't a trail to follow. At one point or another, we had different opinions on which way to go, so we split up.

I ran through the woods, ducking and dodging branches but still bumped into a few of the tree trunks. THUMP. I fell to the ground, with my knees aching and arms covered in dirt. It was a tree's root sticking out of the ground. I glimpsed behind me. *No Zheng.* The moonlight broke through the leaves, accompanied by the sound of crickets and soft rustling from the leaves. I began to second-guess if I should go back.

A frightening thought came into my head. Zheng might have gotten to someone else instead of leaving! I jumped up and dashed back. *Maybe my friends stayed back to fight!* I was drenched in guilt, feeling like a coward and a lousy friend for fleeing.

Bo was alone at where we split earlier.

"Is everyone alright?" I caught my breath.

"I don't know." Bo kept pacing back and forth.

After standing anxiously for what felt like an eternity, Mei came out of the woods. Bo and I gave her a quick hug, grateful that she was safe. Mei asked where Lu and Lingling were, and I gave her the same answer Bo gave me.

No signs of Lingling or Lu. It was dead air, and I knew what everyone was afraid of.

A vague image popped into my head. I was inside a car, and a voice said, "I'll be right back, Cassidy. Don't go anywhere."

Hours passed, day turned to night, and there was still no one coming back.

I was finally fed up with waiting. I pushed open the car door and wandered off.

I had to bring myself back to reality. I felt sick thinking about what may have happened to Lingling and Lu.

"Wait! Did you hear footsteps?" Just after I spoke, Lingling and Lu emerged from the forest! I was relieved. Three of us rushed to give them a bear hug.

Something felt...different. Lingling and Lu were stoic. "Are you okay?" I asked as delicately as possible.

Lingling took a deep breath, then stood a little straighter. "Yes." she choked. "I messed up, an...and Lu almost got killed." Her eyes started to water.

I looked at Lu, whose face was stiff. His glasses fell to the tip of his nose, and he didn't bother to push them up. "Well, you're both safe now. You don't have to worry." *Was that the right thing to say?*

Lingling nodded, not saying another word.

"Are you both okay? Any wounds, or scratches?" Mei asked worriedly.

"You didn't get hurt at all?" Bo added.

"We're fine," Lu muttered.

Obviously, something happened. *Where's Zheng?*

"Do you want to take a break?" Mei asked.

"No, we don't have time. Let's go." Lu and Lingling were sure of it.

Shortly, we set out on the search again. It was hard to believe we were searching for a dragon, which isn't your average late-night chore.

"Why does everything look so wet?" Lu asked hours later. We had gotten a lot of rest on the way here, but it was 3:30 in the morning according to Lingling's windup watch. We were running low on energy.

Lu was right. Leaves on every tree appeared to be shining and dripping. The ground became muddier, but there wasn't a cloud in the sky. You know what? I don't think that helped my case. I probably couldn't see it even if there was a cloud.

"Maybe it's a good sign," Mei said hesitantly. "Dragons usually have control over water, so let's keep going."

"Go where?" Bo asked. There were trees covered in water in every direction, and they seemed to stretch even farther out.

"Well, if we search each way, it's going to take us forever." I yawned.

"That is, if we go together." Lu was hinting at what we should do. It was beyond me that someone who was almost killed wanted to separate in a dangerous forest in the dark. Lu was probably tired. We all were.

"You want to split up?" Bo was not convinced.

"It's the fastest way. We can yell if we need help. I haven't seen any danger for hours!" Lu claimed.

"I cannot even begin to express how many ways it can go wrong!" Bo looked around to see if anyone else was objecting to Lu's idea.

"Whoever thinks we should stay together, raise your hand." Lu took a glance at all of us.

Nobody else raised their hands, except Bo and I. Majority won.

"Okay, everyone goes their separate ways. Please stay in one straight direction." Lingling took over. "Yell for help when needed. Let's meet up again by this pond, in an hour at most." She pointed to a dark pond nearby.

Is it a wise decision? I'm too tired to argue.

THE UNTOLD TRUTH OF CLUB 門神

"Wait, Cassidy, do you want to come with me?" Lingling turned.

"No, I'm fine." Words slipped out of my mouth although my mind told me I'd most likely regret it. I was glad she asked but I wanted to prove that I was capable of doing something alone.

"I'll be right back!" Lingling yelled, waving, and disappearing into the forest. Everyone walked in different directions.

A vague image popped into my head again. *I was inside a car, and a voice said, "I'll be right back, Cassidy. Don't go anywhere."*

Hours passed, day turned to night, and there was still no one coming back.

I was finally fed up with waiting. I pushed open the car door and wandered off.

I roamed around aimlessly. Eventually, I was tired and sat down by a twisted old tree. My eyelids became heavy before everything blacked out.

I refocused myself. *This is not a good idea.* I told myself over and over again. I do like to stay up late, but NOT under these circumstances. I wish I had gone with Lingling, as I had a feeling something was going to happen. I pulled my jacket tighter around myself and turned on my flashlight. My friends had been walking under the moonlight without flashlights to conserve batteries, but I was afraid to walk alone in the dark. Every sound in the forest could be from a predator.

I hadn't even been alone for a minute before my breath quickened, my heart raced, and my palms were sweaty. Nevertheless, I forced myself to take another step, and another.

It was only five minutes in when things started to go wrong. I walked down a path, when an object that wasn't supposed to be there caught my eye. It was a piece of white cloth.

A minute or two passed when I saw a piece of white cloth again. I kept on walking, thinking these people would have a lot to retrace their steps if they got lost. Even after coming up with a theory like that, a part of me still couldn't help but wonder, *is that the same piece?* My mind kept questioning as I was getting close to yet another white cloth.

It was my third time seeing it. I kept walking.

After five more times of sighting, it took all my willpower to refrain myself from picking it up. I remembered Ms. Wu's warning about not picking up suspicious objects. In Chinese mythology, there are so many mysterious and dangerous things.

It only took three more sightings for my willpower to give in. *You know what? Maybe the white cloth is here for a reason. It might give me clues to find the dragon and I can't miss the opportunity.* I slowed down toward a white cloth hesitantly. I stopped, bent down, and picked up a corner of the white cloth with two fingers.

With an unimaginable speed, the white cloth wrapped around my entire hand! It began to pull me toward where I came from with an invisible force. It was like the cloth had its own mind and strength. No matter how hard I resisted and tried to pull myself away, the cloth continued to drag me.

The cloth started to increase its speed, while I attempted in vain to plant my feet sturdy on the ground to free myself. Nothing I did dampened its speed even a bit. I struggled with the cloth relentlessly.

"Help!" I yelled.

The cloth accelerated to a point where I had to run if I didn't want to be dragged to death. In the distance, I heard my friends running and shouting my name. Suddenly, the white cloth made a sharp right turn heading straight toward the pond. I finally realized what the cloth wanted. It wanted me to drown.

I was horrified. *How deep is the pond?* Turned out, a lot deeper than I wished. My feet were in the water. My neck was in the water. My head was in the water. The screams from my friends became muffled then diminished. I didn't get a chance to gulp down air before my head went under. I was never good at holding my breath. I can hold maybe thirty seconds at most.

Ten seconds. All I focused on was to grab on anything with my other hand to resist the force.

Sixteen seconds. The cloth stopped moving, but only because it couldn't go any deeper.

Twenty-one seconds. I tried to rip the cloth, but the fabric felt indestructible.

Twenty-seven seconds. I wanted to cry. I wanted to breathe air so badly.

Thirty seconds. I made my last-ditch effort. Since the cloth wanted me to die, I stopped fighting and let myself float, with all my muscles loose and my chest screaming. As soon as my body touched the bottom of the pond, the grip on my wrist loosened. The white cloth quickly floated away from me.

I frantically kicked back up to the surface, taking in a big mouthful of air.

"Cassidy!" The voices rang in my ear.

I was too exhausted. At the worst possible moment, my muscles gave up on me. My arms and legs were unable to move any longer. I started to sink.

"Help!" I yelled before my head was under water *again*.

Suddenly, something grabbed my wrist firmly. *The White Cloth!* I tried to pull away in vain. *Faking death probably won't work this time. I'm going to die.*

Surprisingly, I was being pulled up instead of being dragged down. I broke through the surface, gasping for air. It was Lingling! She threw me on her back and swam to the land. No words could describe how grateful I was. I escaped death by mere seconds!

Once I sat down, I took shaky breaths and tried to pull myself together. Everyone gathered around me and swarmed me with questions.

"Cassidy, are you okay?" It was all I could hear coming from every direction.

"I'm fine." My voice was still weak.

"Are you sure?" asked Mei.

"Yes." Even though it was a traumatizing experience, I was physically okay except for the coughs.

Mei proceeded to repeat the same question twenty times, adding *are you sure* to the beginning.

"It's amazing you got away," Bo said in wonder after Mei finally finished and I stopped coughing. "A creature that'll drown you if you dare to pick it up. I think it's the White Cloth Demon. Yeah, it sounds right. How did you get away? I heard it'll only let you go after you're dead."

"I pretended to be dead," I uttered.

Everyone started murmuring, like yeah that makes sense, and whoa she's a genius. Okay they didn't say that, but I imagined it.

"How did you even think of something like that?" Lu said in admiration.

I shrugged my shoulders. I honestly didn't know. The idea came to me.

"Lingling and I tried to use our power to part the water for you, but you were sinking too fast! So, Lingling dove in."

Surrounded by my friends, I started to feel better after getting over the shock. Then out of nowhere, a sense of embarrassment overtook my emotions. I caused such commotion. I hoped my friends would never ask me why I picked up that White Cloth. *What was I even thinking?*

"Why are you all together?" I decided to steer away from the subject. "I thought we were supposed to take separate ways?"

"Lu yelled something, so we came back," Bo explained.

"Why did you yell, Lu? You still haven't told us," Mei asked.

"Follow me." Lu was beaming. "I think I've found the dragon."

We grinned and *air-applauded* silently. Lu reminded us to turn off flashlights to avoid waking up the dragon.

On the way there, I scanned for Lingling. Surprisingly, I found her alone behind a tree facing away. In her hands was the pot shaped like a squeezed pumpkin. *Why now?* Of course, she wasn't washing her face. Not wanting to sneak behind her, I quickly turned away.

Soon I heard thuds coming from her direction. "Thank you, Lingling, for saving me." I waited until she caught up with me.

"Of course. I'd never let you drown." Lingling gave me a reassuring smile.

Lu led us into a large flat area. The ground was coated in water. *Why does it have to be water again!* Around the seemingly shallow pond was a barrier of trees. There was just enough room for us to squeeze through. Through the top, the wind was gushing in. You could see many, many brilliant stars, where sun rays would be shining. Not now of course. Bo looked up at the nightly sky, starstruck by the stars.

"How do you know the dragon is here?" Mei whispered.

"Over there," Lu said, pointing to one of the large boulders. I squinted but saw nothing.

"That's the dragon," Lu said as if it was obvious.

I took a closer look. The details started becoming clearer as my eyes adjusted to the darkness. Scales, slight movements, sharp claws, and puffs of breath every few seconds. The dragon was curled up in a ball. I was in awe.

"I don't want to be disrespectful to the dragon," Lingling whispered, "but I think the only way to get its scale is to take it forcefully."

Without being asked, Lu quietly unzipped his bag and took out a knife. He slowly approached the dragon. Either the scale was really tough, or the knife was really dull because it didn't seem like Lu made any progress. In the meantime, the dragon could wake up at any moment.

"Can't you go a little faster?" I whispered encouragingly when Lu stopped briefly from cutting. Lu shrugged his shoulders and continued.

Suddenly, the dragon shifted position, making ripples of water around it. We quickly backed away like little birds.

The dragon slowly rose to full height.

"Who dares to enter my sanctuary?" the dragon bellowed, speaking the iconic entry line of any dragon. *It's usually a cave, but still....* My admiration morphed into fear.

"Sorry, we were exploring and got lost. We'll leave now," Lingling turned, keeping a calm tone.

The dragon turned his head aimlessly. "Don't think you can get away because I'm blind. Why are you here?" *Blind?*

"We're here for one of your scales," Lu said boldly. That didn't help our case. *By the way, we're here to steal your scale. Are you going to kill us now?*

"We need it for medicine," Mei seconded.

"Medicine? I don't give out my scales."

"What can we do to get it?" Lu responded in an instant.

"Do-you-know what you asked, little boy?" The dragon appeared to be annoyed. "I can ask for anything in the world for my scales. Choose your words carefully next time. Otherwise, you'll regret it."

The dragon puffed and continued, "Anyway, now that I think of it, I do have a little errand you can run for me in exchange. I have a friend, who resides in Mount Nanhu, on the island of Taiwan. It's my friend's turn to visit me for a reunion. Frankly, I don't think it remembers where I live. It's losing memory. I can't get there either because I've been blind for some time. You may bring my friend here. Do you accept my request?"

We stared at the dragon dumbfoundedly. You don't meet a mythical creature, then hear it rambling about a request every day.

"How do we find it?" Bo asked.

The dragon blew water out of his mouth in a spiral shape onto one of the thick trees. It was a very detailed scene. In the center was an enormous mountain surrounded by a trail of smaller peaks, kind of shaped like a cone.

"This is the best I can describe." The dragon blew once more, which marked an X on the lower part of the mountain. "This is a mental picture of where my friend lives from what I can remember."

"How far is it?" I asked.

"It'll take you a few hours to get there no matter which type of transportation you take. If you want *my* scale, you better get going now." The dragon went into a rest position again. "Do you accept my request?"

Lu said without any hesitation, "*Yes*, we do."

CHAPTER 14:
AN UNEXPECTED FRIEND

February 6 (Tuesday 7:30 am)

I woke up to a loud *water* breaking bang and sudden impact! My eyes shot open to the sight of our boat in mid-air. The impact lurched me up from my seat. The boat barely landed right side up on the water, making a huge splash.

"我的天啊!" Bo yelled desperately (meaning *my sky*).

I turned my neck. There was a pointy rock behind us. *No, no, no!* I thought Bo was supposed to watch our boat! I grasped the wood so tightly that my knuckles turned white, like it would help. There was a crack at the tip of the boat where it was hit by the rock. I watched in despair as the crack slowly crept from the bow to the stern. It was obvious there was no way we could stop the cracking and the inevitable doom of this boat.

In a matter of seconds, the crack extended to the stern. Our boat fell apart into pieces in a blink of an eye. We hit the water with many loud gasps. At least, each of us grabbed a piece of wood as a floating device.

Oh, the water is really, really cold! I had to admit I panicked when I was in the water ONCE AGAIN. A life-threatening event like the White Cloth incident does that to you. I couldn't believe it. Bo must have fallen asleep during his shift watching the boat. I remember it kept drifting to the right earlier because of the high tide. It probably got too close and hit one of the rocks.

"I'll do the fire spell," Lu yelled. "Who's doing it after me? I can't do it forever!"

"I will." Bo, Lingling and Mei answered simultaneously.

Instantly, I felt warm pins and needles surrounding me.

A small island was in sight, thankfully not too far away. The wind smacked our faces as we held onto the wood like floaties in cold water. Even with a plank, Bo was desperately kicking water trying to stabilize himself. In the process, he splashed salty water in everyone's eyes.

All of us made it to the island safely.

"Bo, how did you let our boat hit the rock? I thought you were watching it!" I lashed out as soon as I got a chance. "We can't finish the mission now!"

"I'm sorry." Bo apologized profusely, pulling his bushy hair, "I can't believe it. I reminded myself over and over and over to stay awake. I must've closed my eyes before I had a chance to wake up the next person."

Multiple sighs.

"We can't go anywhere now." Lu slumped.

"Principal Jiang asked us to take good care of this boat, but we destroyed it!" Lingling yelled, followed by a groan.

"I know," Bo mumbled, looking down at his shoes.

"Don't feel too bad, Bo." Mei looked at us, signaling us to agree with her. "I mean I could easily doze off too. Right?"

Now it was Bo's turn to sigh. After a moment of silence, I felt bad yelling at Bo. If it was my shift, I might've fallen asleep too.

"Sorry Bo," I apologized.

"Sorry," Lu and Lingling murmured.

"No worries. I shouldn't have fallen asleep."

It was sunrise. The island was covered in lush green trees with rolling hills in the distance, tinted in red from the rays. A white shack was nearby, with some littered cans around it. Beyond the shack was a road with a narrow sidewalk and an old green fence. According to the map and Lu, we landed on a small island called Juguang Township, one of the Matsu Islands.

"People live here! What if they call the authorities on us?" I said, thinking out loud.

"Then we won't complete our quest in time," Lu said depressingly.

A series of groans came from every direction.

"Do we even have enough food left?" Mei rubbed her forehead.

"Let's check." Lingling opened her backpack immediately.

A bit of good news was that we still had a day's worth of food and water left, along with clothes, first aid kits, a working flashlight that might run out of batteries at any time, and some other small items.

I couldn't help but worry. We didn't have lots of supplies left, there was no transportation to get us out of this island, and we couldn't ask for help from locals either. *Now what?* My mind was blank. The mood was dreary.

"We have to get off this island as soon as possible," Lu said while kicking sand under his feet. Nothing in his voice sounded reassuring.

"Do you think we can find a boat here?" Bo suggested with a frown.

Suddenly, Mei's eyes lit up. "I know how to build one! I've done it in the fight class. The floor turned to water, and I used the logs around me to make one."

I could tell from her little smile that she was very proud of herself.

"All right! Mei will build the raft." Lingling made the call as usual. "Four of us will gather the materials."

We decided to reuse the planks from our last boat that were still in good condition, hoping the new raft would keep the same speed as before. If not, our quest would be in big trouble. Mei gave us a verbal list of things we needed to collect, like baby saplings (even though she didn't want them to be hurt) to tie logs together, and flat sturdy logs.

"Let's separate into two groups and spread out. Make sure you don't let the locals see us!" Lingling started to walk toward the right, asking Lu to join her. To my surprise, Lu walked straight to the left, not even looking at Lingling. He mumbled something like he wanted to check out the other side.

Bo offered to pair up with Lingling, which left me with Lu. I never really talked to Lu much, so we walked in awkward silence at first.

THE UNTOLD TRUTH OF CLUB 門神

A note to self: What to Do with Awkward Silence

Sometimes, to break the awkward silence is to start the conversation by addressing it. Make it clear that it's awkward, and it's fine. Laughing or having emotions is helpful too. If you don't address it, it may stay that way, or get better over time. By the way, I didn't need to address the awkwardness here because a frog apparently saved the day! Read on-it'll make sense. Note: This advice is from a thirteen-year-old, not a professional, so take it at your own risk.

Resume the story.

After Lu and I finished the heavy lifting of picking out logs, we were scanning the ground for suitable baby saplings. When I pulled up a baby sapling, I jerked. Something leaped off the stick. I was not expecting it.

"What?" Lu asked.

"I..." I squinted at the ground. "Oh, it's just a frog."

"Where?"

"Right there," I said, pointing to the frog that was very obvious to me. It was lime green with various brown spots.

"I still don't see it." So far, an extremely *dull* conversation.

I picked up a stick, pointing at the frog with its tip only an inch away. "There!" I poked it. The frog leaped a few inches, making the leaves shift.

"Oh well, it's pretty obvious now." Lu went down on his knees, poking it with a stick too.

"Don't let Mei know we're doing this." I smiled, recalling my conversation with Mei when she practiced her spell on a frog.

"Definitely not." Lu smiled back. "Do you know we are supposed to dissect frogs next year?"

"Oh no, Mei is going to be so mad at the science teacher!"

Both of us laughed, picturing what Mei was going to act like. We probably shouldn't laugh at her, but I have to say it felt good to laugh like that! The awkwardness slowly faded away.

The frog hopped a few times and landed next to a distinctive rock that I overlooked. I picked it up and turned it around a few times. The rock was yellow with a swirl of white, mostly flat, and a little jagged around the edges. It seemed like something Lu would be interested in, so I handed the stone to him.

Lu's eyes widened. "You know what? This rock looks very similar to the one my dad gave me," Lu said lightheartedly.

"Where did the frog..."

I was halfway through my sentence but, *what did Lu just say? His dad? I thought you have to be an orphan at the age of two in order to become a Menshen. How could Lu remember his dad at that age?*

"Oh, my dad came to the orphanage when we were seven to bring us home." Lu must have noticed my reaction. I didn't even have to ask! It would be nice if it happened like that all the time. Sometimes I feel like I annoy people with my many, many questions.

I remembered my conversation with Lingling by the pond. *She said her parents died in an earthquake when they were infants, so their dad...didn't die? I don't see how this makes sense unless either Lingling or Lu isn't telling the truth.*

THE UNTOLD TRUTH OF CLUB 門神

Although I wanted to know what happened to their dad, I didn't press it. I learned my lesson with Lingling last time. Besides, I was in too much of a good mood to natter about something serious. I simply nodded my head and carried on with baby saplings.

Once we collected enough logs and baby saplings, we headed back. I dropped some saplings along the way. After several attempts to pick one up, but ended up dropping more in the process, I gave up on the ones that fell. I also got a rock of my own and put it under my chin. I wasn't starting a rock collection, but Lu offered it to me.

Soon I saw Mei, next to a pile of logs. She was sitting on her knees and cutting the excess part of a log. "Hey, can you help me? I need to cut off twigs poking out of the logs." Mei looked at us.

We took out knives from our backpacks and began to cut.

"So, how are things going with raft building?" Lu asked while cutting.

"Well, turns out I forgot this raft isn't for one person. It's for five. So I'm going to need more wood than I thought," Mei said bitterly. "I'll be done soon. Just go kill more baby saplings after you finish that log."

Lu and I continued to make more trips until Mei said we had enough, so did Bo and Lingling.

Mei insisted she was almost done and asked the four of us to take a break. We sat down and watched the waves rolling back and forth. The sun was hot, giving me a slight sunburn. At the side, Bo was fiddling with a small object in his hand that deflected the sunlight.

"What's that, Bo?" I asked.

"Well, I think it's a silver plate, but I don't know exactly how it works." Bo held up a pocket-sized, circular plate with a silver rim. "Do you remember I was away for a trip right before you came to our school?"

"Yes." *Right, I meant to ask him about that three-week trip.*

"I was on a quest to bring supplies to the moon goddess, Chang'e. Her rabbit craved earth carrots," Bo said, noticing how weird that sounded to me. "A group of us was tasked to find Qingniao (青鸟) on the peak of Kunlun Mountain. It's a special bird from the Queen Mother of the West. This bird would deliver carrot seeds and gardening supplies to Chang'e."

"So...the silver plate?" I asked, choosing not to ask how the moon goddess's rabbit made a request of earth food, or how carrots grew on the moon. At this point, I wasn't surprised to hear the famous moon goddess legend was real, but growing carrots on the moon? It was out of my imagination.

"After we found Qingniao and gave the supplies to the bird, it flew into thick vines and got stuck," Bo continued. "I spent at least an hour untangling the vines and set Qingniao free. Sometime later on our way back, Qingniao flew back and gave me this. I guess it must be a gift from the moon goddess for saving Qingniao."

"Does it have any power?" I was intrigued.

"I'm still experimenting with it," Bo said with childlike wonder but using words a child would not. "I figured out that the silver plate can deflect sunlight in a powerful manner. If I point it to a spot in a certain way, that spot becomes heated. Before I can confidently use it as a weapon,

I need to try many conditions like combinations of angle, distance, and duration. I carry the plate around every day just in case situations arise. You never know."

"Maybe a situation like using it as a mirror to fix your hair. Will that be helpful?" Mei said with a smirk while continuing her raft-making.

I laughed lightly. I didn't even mind Bo's rambling because I was in a good mood. Nothing dangerous happened on the island, unless I count a cute tiny frog as dangerous, or light rain. Did I mention that it started to rain? Well, it drizzled after the clouds moved in.

The raft was finally completed. There were ten logs laying in parallel. On top of it were two logs, one on each end strapped perpendicularly with baby saplings. The raft was a lot heavier than I thought. We managed to pull it across the sand to the water in the misty rain, carefully stepping on the raft one by one without tipping it over.

To our relief, the raft did a great jolt once again! I guess using the planks from our old boat was a good idea after all. Without a top, the ride was quite wet and windy, to say the least. The mixture of wind and water drops kept hitting my face.

The remainder of the trip felt a lot shorter. We saw land in less than ten minutes, which seriously confused Lu. He said we shouldn't have reached land for another couple of hours. Nevertheless, we slowed down. By that time, the rain had stopped, but the clouds still covered the sky.

Nearby, a spotted seal swam fast toward us. It stopped right next to me. Naturally, I reached out to touch it because it was so cute. You would think I learned my lesson after the white cloth incident, but a seal in the ocean didn't raise any alarm to me.

"DON'T TOUCH SHEN!" shouted Bo. Everyone turned to look at him in surprise. They were also admiring the cute seal, or Shen, as Bo put it. *Are there even spotted seals near Taiwan?*

"Raft! Get away from Shen!" Bo commanded the raft, but the raft didn't work that way. To be honest, I had no idea how it worked.

While we were mesmerized by the seal, a violent force struck the other side of the raft. We plummeted into the water.

WATER AGAIN? I was completely caught off guard and swallowed a mouthful of salty water. The newly built raft became loose and separated apart. *We just built it!* My mind was filled with a surge of frustration, clouding my fear for a second.

Shen looked like a horned serpent and resembled a crocodile with a red mane and scales crawling inward along its spine. It roared and dove straight toward us. For a second, we forgot about Bo, who was scared out of his mind, splashing water like crazy. Lu grabbed Bo's arm to keep him afloat.

Shen emerged from the water surface. It kept circling around us and spewing vapor. We scattered as far as we could.

Shen dove underwater once more. I could see it through the water, but it was hazy. Shen suddenly sped up, gaining speed with every millisecond, *aiming right at me.* I swam away as fast as I could, like grabbing on an imaginary rope.

It looks crazy, it feels crazy, and it is *crazy.*

CRASH. Shen broke the surface. I was sure I would die. The tough scales of the beast grazed my jacket. Suddenly, my backpack was gone, though my spear was spared. I turned my head only to see Shen shredding my backpack then swallowed my last box of ham. I was speechless.

"Meat," Shen said in a deep raspy voice, sounding like it hadn't drunk water in a thousand years. "More meat." The hoarse voice boomed in my ears, becoming more furious by the second.

"Does anyone have any ham left?" Bo whispered. We shook our heads.

Shen stared straight at me.

Say something! My mouth felt dry and my head screamed. Never had I found it so hard to speak. I sensed everyone was looking at me, waiting for me to say something. Pushing aside my fears, I finally shouted, "We…we don't have any more ham, but I promise I'll get you more."

"Do it."

"But I'll need you to give us a ride." Apparently, I was bolder than I ever imagined. *Why not ask? We don't have any other transportations.*

Shen didn't speak for a moment. I stared at it anxiously, hoping that the deadly dragon would take up my offer. Finally, it snarled, "Come."

For a second, I thought my idea worked but…*can Shen be trusted?* I started to doubt if I was making us to be the meal Shen wanted after all.

Before I knew it, my friends quickly swam towards Shen while mouthing "thank you" to me. Feeling encouraged, I followed them with every ounce of energy I had left. I pushed myself up and clung to the scales. To my amazement, it had some sort of magnetic force.

"Where to?" Shen asked once we settled down.

"Mount Nanhu. We'll get your ham on our way," Lingling said boldly. Shen didn't move a bit.

"Where to, Meat Holder?" Shen repeated, looking at me directly.

"Mo...Mount Nanhu." *Meat Holder? This is the strangest name I've ever been called.* This time, Shen swam off.

Shen didn't listen to Lingling, but to me, Meat Holder. *Why?* Sitting on a dragon and trying to find another dragon to reunite with a blind dragon who hated the way Lu spoke. *Yep, definitely normal.*

At first, I felt like riding on a mechanical bull, although I've only seen it in movies. The bumpiness only lasted for a few minutes, then the wind slowed down to a point where it was simply a gentle breeze.

Thanks to Shen, our new "friend", we traveled much faster than our boat or raft. As Bo explained, Shen can create mirages, and that was why we saw the land and seal earlier. Mei added that Shen can shapeshift, so it must have done that to morph seats for us. Shen grunted in response to all of this.

Racing on the waves, I was thrilled. The mist of water coated my face. Even though we were traveling just above the water surface, I felt like flying.

At one point, I forgot why I was here. I thought about my life before this crazy quest, and whether it was ever going to be the same again. I faintly missed my old life in my last orphanage. I missed Monk Taiyuan and my old friends who I grew up with since I was five. *I probably won't see them again.*

Of course, I like the excitement and powers I have been exposed to lately, but sometimes this new life scares me.

CHAPTER 15:
BO'S REDEMPTION
February 7 (Wednesday 3:30 am)

I asked Shen to land on the rocky shore. The mountains were gigantic under the moonlight, with trees and plants swarming the bottom. *A leafy mountain.* As the altitude went up, fewer and fewer plants existed, eventually leading to a bare and rocky summit.

We hiked for a few hours. It was an uncomfortable walk, even without a backpack (thanks to Shen). Not because it was dark, but because my feet were wet. Why? Shen was a water dragon, so it had to land in the water at least five meters away from shore. My shoes were soaking wet, but I had to keep them on because of the rough surface. I would say the squeaking sound was somehow satisfying.

It was finally sunrise. I saw the bumpy road we were on, with a forest on the left and bumps of mountains on the right.

"I don't see the rock formation anywhere," Bo said hopelessly for the one hundredth time, glancing at the large mountains.

"We'll find it soon," Lu said, also for the one hundredth time.

THE UNTOLD TRUTH OF CLUB 門神

"But how? Half of this place is made up of mountains!" Lingling exclaimed.

"Bo, where does Nanhu mountain start exactly?" Mei asked skeptically. She was the only person who hadn't said anything yet. I found it kind of funny how we took turns to talk.

"I don't know. I'm not the map guy," Bo said.

"Well, technically, the mountains started thousands of years ago." I kidded.

Mei chuckled, then sighed. "I can't believe we've been looking for hours!"

"We'll find it soon," Lu repeated one hundred and one times.

"But you've been saying that for hours!" Mei responded.

"Oh no." Bo suddenly realized something. "That picture of the mountain is from the dragon's point of view, from up above!" He threw his hands up in exasperation. "We'll never know the exact location because we look at it from a lower perspective. That could be it for all we know!" Bo pointed to a small bump in the distance that looked nothing like the image we saw.

Being bummed out, everyone sighed and sat down on the rails at the side of the road. It seemed hopeless. We had been looking for hours and hours for this rock formation. So far, we were able to manage every situation, but maybe not this time. I looked at everything around me, like little holes in the leaves outlined by a brown color. Then I picked at the rust formed on the steel railing.

Did you ever play a hide-and-seek game where someone hid really well? You kept looking, but it felt quiet and eerie and you wanted to call off the game. That's what it felt like, except nobody could call it off because it wasn't a game.

It's a five-hour ride going back to the dragon. Then what? Ask the dragon the exact location? Does it even know? After that, it'll be another five hours each way! It's probably going to be too late to save Pingye. What should we do?

"We're not sitting here," Lu said sternly, "Pingye is dying. What do we do about it?" Nobody answered. "Let's cross options off the list. One, it's almost impossible to find the mountain but we can keep trying." Lu stopped, while everyone shrugged. "Two, we can go back to the dragon, ask for specific directions and come back."

"We may run out of time if we do that. Fifteen hours." Lingling brought it up in a pessimistic tone.

I stopped picking at the rust and focused on thinking. *We need to find the dragon's friend in order to get the scale, but we don't know where it is. Without the scale, Pingye dies.* I was reliving our encounter with the dragon. *Last time when Lu tried to take the scale, it didn't work. But could it? A scale is what we needed, isn't it? We don't need to find the dragon's friend. We just need a scale.*

"How about we don't bring back the dragon friend," I said quietly, "but only take the scale?"

"Yes!" Lu jumped up.

"It's dangerous," Bo warned, "but it could work."

"Well, the dragon woke up last time. If it finds out we betrayed its offer, it'll smash us as if we were little bugs." Mei exaggerated with hand gestures.

"Don't make us sound like the bad guys!" Lu said loudly, "The dragon knows we're desperate and willing to do anything to save our friend. It took advantage of us for its own benefit. The dragon made the deal sound amazing... finding a friend in exchange for the scale, but Pingye's life is on the line! If it's a good person...er... dragon, it'll give us a scale, with the benefit of knowing someone's life is saved." I had never seen Lu speak so much at once.

"We already failed!" Lingling yelled back. "If we betray the dragon, it might not hesitate to kill us this time! By the way, what makes the dragon so bad? It only wanted to see its friend!"

"No one else can help find its friend?" Lu insisted.

"Oh yeah, you're absolutely right. Maybe a nice little bird will stop by!" Lingling said sarcastically.

"Stop, both of you." Mei interrupted them calmly. "Lingling, thank you for trying to see the good in people...er...dragons, but we don't have much time. If we go back to ask for the location again, it'll be another fifteen hours. Pingye may die. We don't want to take that risk. Hopefully, we'll take its scale and get out of there before it kills us.

"Besides, sometimes you have to break the rules to do the right thing, even if it's a rule from a dragon." Mei was certainly not the first one to say that. We all hear it in movies, books, and even kids' stories about rules.

Lingling sighed. "I'm still not completely on board but we *do* need to get going." She paused for a second then said, "First of all, we need a plan."

It was five hours later when we landed. The sun was beaming down on us. I kept thinking about the plan we made, wondering how it would turn out. Guided by Lu's compass, we spent an hour locating the blind dragon. My heart was racing while we walked by the familiar pond. The White Cloth Demon flashed through my mind.

"There it is," I whispered. The dragon was napping in a sitting position on the shallow water. I couldn't believe we were at the exact place yesterday.

Lingling took out an empty water bottle, put a portion of our precious food inside the water bottle, and mixed it with water. She doused Lu with the mix. Trust me, this was all part of the plan. Yes, it was a weird plan.

We adapted it from another military strategy book called "Thirty-six Stratagems" written in the sixth century. The sixth strategy is called 声东击西, which means to mislead the enemy by surprise. Literally speaking, it says to threaten the east but strike the west.

Lu stepped toward the dragon, holding his knife. He insisted on doing it by himself again. Once Lu's foot touched the water and made a tiny splash, the dragon jerked. It was snarling, crouching, and started to approach him. Lu flew to the right side of the dragon, with his steps splashing water around him.

At the same time, Lingling spread the rest of the food-containing water and mimicked footsteps on the left side of the dragon. This way, both sides of the dragon sounded the same and smelt the same, *at least we hoped so.*

The dragon began swinging its claws at *both* sides, missing Lu by inches. Lu paused briefly in the water, so the dragon focused its attention on the left side with louder fake footsteps. Lingling increased the noises, while Lu sneaked closer to the right side of the dragon.

It wasn't easy, with the dragon moving and all, but Lu was able to stand right next to the dragon. The second when his blade touched the scale, the dragon turned around and bellowed, "It's *you* again!"

We froze at the sound of rage from the dragon. It was like being caught by an orphanage worker, or parents in other cases. This wasn't part of the plan. We were supposed to run away as soon as Lu got the scale.

Our plan… almost worked.

"We had a fair deal, and yet you tried to steal my scale!" The dragon was furious.

Lu sprinted back, while the rest of us stood in silence, wondering if we should speak or move at all.

"SPEAK! I know you're there. Yes, I can smell you, all five of you. It was a simple, simple deal. You lead my friend here, and I give you my scale. It's easy, is it not?"

"You took advantage of us," Lu said with conviction, "when you knew we would do anything to save our friend's life."

"We tried very hard, but you gave no clear directions!" Mei shouted.

The dragon didn't respond. When another human becomes silent during an argument with you, it usually means you've won. But with a dragon, the silence could mean it's plotting to kill you.

"Who are you, youngsters (小鬼)?" The dragon asked word by word. *Really? Among all the words in the dictionary, it chose youngsters?*

"We're Menshens." Lingling spoke up proudly.

"Mmm, Menshens," The dragon said slowly, as if in deep thought. "I remember one. It was a few hundred years ago at the Yin Shan mountains."

We exchanged a glance at each other, being drawn into the dragon's story.

"What happened?" The words slipped out of my mouth.

Like a flood gate of memories was broken down, the dragon started. "One day, I was taking an afternoon nap when someone shook me awake. She started rambling about a giant beast coming my way any moment. I listened. Soon enough, a beast with sharp claws jumped out behind trees. It was a furious fight. Even with only one arm, she was one of the best fighters I remember."

My jaw dropped. *The One-Armer? I can't believe it.*

The dragon puffed a few times before it continued, "Fast as a cheetah, strong as a tiger. That's how she was. I fought hard, but she was really one of a kind. She whirled through the air like a cyclone, spinning and swinging her spear at the beast. She never backed off once. Nothing on this planet could scare her away."

I was in a daze. It sounded like a scene from a Kung Fu movie.

"The beast hurled itself at her. She dodged every time. Yet another attack from the beast, she jumped over it before it fell on its face. She turned around in an instant and jabbed her spear on the beast's back. It looked dead, only I didn't expect the beast to jump back up suddenly and stab its claws at my eyes."

The dragon winced as if it was still in pain. "Luckily, she pulled out the spear from its back and kept jabbing until it dropped to the ground, dead. Thankfully, I was alive but I lost my eyesight ever since."

"It must be Hao," Lingling whispered to us in awe.

THE UNTOLD TRUTH OF CLUB 門神

The dragon was still deep in its memory lane. "She didn't want anything in return. She said she was a Menshen and only needed directions to Oyu Tolgoi."

"Was this Menshen by any chance named Hao?" Bo asked delicately.

"She said call me *One-Armer*."

I was captivated by the story. *Hao was amazing, but why did she steal books from the Underground library? It didn't make sense.*

"All right," The dragon came back to the present. "I like Menshens. Let me give you another chance. If you complete my new request, I will give you the scale you wanted. All five of you will be free to go."

"If you don't, you shall search for my friend again until you find it. Your choice. Don't worry, this request won't take long, or not."

"Let's try and make it short," Bo whispered to the rest of us.

"Agreed." Lu clutched onto his knife.

"What is your request?" Lingling asked boldly.

"Make me walk over to you."

That was it. *Making the dragon walk over to us.* It sounded so simple, but not at the same time. We gathered in a circle.

"It's obviously a test of intelligence," I whispered.

"Huh?" Mei said, "I was thinking along the line of pushing it."

Lu quickly turned to face the dragon, with his arms extended and ready to go.

"Wait, Lu! I'm sure there's something else we can do other than pushing it," Lingling whispered.

"I don't think we can force it to walk." I was wracking my brain. "We need to trick it. It's a dragon after all!"

Lu dropped his arms. All eyes were on Bo. He was staring at the ground with his bushy eyebrows scrunched up. Finally, he said, "I think... I read something like this in a history book. A similar situation happened between an Emperor and a smart scholar. The scholar ended up tricking the emperor successfully. I don't know if it'll work on a dragon, but I'll give it a try unless you have other ideas."

We looked at each other and shook heads.

"Go for it. We trust you," Lu encouraged. I trust Bo too. It's just that I hope he would make his speech succinct because dragons probably won't have patience listening to someone rambling.

Without saying another word, Bo took a step forward facing the dragon who was ten meters away from us. "I am Bo Chen," He introduced himself. "I *can't* make you walk over to me."

What? I didn't expect Bo to start like that.

"But I can make you walk from where I'm standing to where you are now," Bo said confidently, facing the dragon.

"Try," said the dragon before walking to Bo.

"Now, how do you make me walk back to where I was?" The dragon asked, standing next to Bo.

"Well..." Bo paused for a second. "I can't make you walk back to where you were before."

What? How is this going to work? I could see the dragon was getting annoyed.

"However, I have fulfilled your request of making you walk over to me."

THE UNTOLD TRUTH OF CLUB 門神

Wow. Bo's speech was surprisingly short and to the point, not even one extra word! I was impressed. In a way, this is his redemption after wrecking our boat. That is, if the dragon kept its promise.

The dragon stood in silence and stayed planted in the same spot. We waited patiently. *Tick tock. Tick tock*. I was getting more and more anxious with every second that passed.

Finally, the dragon spoke. "Use it well, and save a life." It shook off a piece of scale and blew it to us. In a flash, Lu single-handedly caught the scale like catching a ping pong ball.

"You only have eighteen hours to use it." The dragon walked back to where he was. "The power of my scale only lasts eighteen hours after it's taken off. You will not get another one."

We didn't stay a second longer and raced straight back. Once the dragon was out of sight, we burst out laughing and congratulated each other again and again. I couldn't help jumping up and down. What a relief! We got the scale after all.

"I can't believe this is all it took, after spending so much time searching for the dragon friend!" I exclaimed while we were heading back.

"And it's because of Bo," Mei said.

Lu flashed an overdone smile at Bo.

"Well, it's actually because of One-Armer." Bo brushed it off.

"I wish I could fight like her," Lingling said in admiration.

"Me too! We're supposed to learn Kung Fu next year. I can't wait!" Lu couldn't contain his excitement. He bent his knees and struck a perfect horse-riding stance. Everyone, even myself, followed him and burst out laughing.

We kept speed walking. Bo lingered behind looking like he was in his thinking mode again.

"Are you reflecting on your hero moment, Bo?" Mei joked.

"Hmm...I wonder what made Hao steal the ancient texts from the Underground library. Why was she looking for Oyu Tolgoi? I don't even know where Oyu Tolgoi is."

"Me either." Lingling suddenly realized something. "Speaking of the missing books, did anyone ever find out what the riddle means?"

"I did." Bo grinned with pride. "It's about the Kuril Islands, a chain of volcano islands located north of Japan."

Lingling's eyes widened in wonder. Her mouth opened as if about to say something. Instead, she broke out into an ear-to-ear smile.

"Thank you, Bo." Lu exchanged a smile with Lingling.

We hurried back to where we started. To my delight, Shen was there patiently waiting for us.

"Don't forget we only have eighteen hours to use the scale. Not to mention we still need to find the lotus flower seeds." I reminded everyone.

"Cassidy is right." Lingling peeped at her watch and announced, "No matter what, we have to be back to school before midnight tomorrow."

"Based on my calculation, it shouldn't be a problem." Lu said confidently.

"If nothing unexpected happens...." Bo added.

"We'll make it work." Lu was sure of it.

This was no doubt the most important victory I ever experienced since I joined the Paiya Boarding School. But the mission was hardly over yet.

CHAPTER 16:
TRUTH MONSTER
February 7 (Wednesday 12:30 pm)

On the way to Nasha wetland, we made a few quick stops looking for ham but to no avail. None of the stops was worth mentioning, except this one.

Guided by Lu and his map, I asked Shen to take a right turn and drop us off. Minutes later, a city appeared among the mountains. Shen landed close to the rocky shore and let us off. As soon as we got on our feet, it dove into the water and disappeared.

"Is Shen coming back?" Mei asked in a worried voice.

"I sure hope so." Lu tried to rationalize the situation. "It wants ham, right?"

I nodded. "The best thing we can do is to find the ham. Maybe Shen wants to take a break."

Looking around, I spotted an old man with a dog staring at us from not too far away. Imagine seeing a strange creature like Shen! While I stood frozen, my friends quickly took charge of the situation.

"Mei," Bo sighed as if they had done it a thousand times.

"Yeah, I know." Mei walked up to the old man and looked straight into his eyes. The old man seemed at a loss

THE UNTOLD TRUTH OF CLUB 門神

for words, like how I was when I first learned about Menshen. His dog kept jumping up and down to Mei and barking continuously. A minute later, the old man blinked a few times, looked away, and started walking with his dog.

"So," I said at last.

"I erased his memory for ten minutes before and after." Mei yawned, rubbing her eyes.

I stared at the man who was walking away. *This is crazy.* I mean anything could happen at that moment and he wouldn't remember a thing of it. If he fell and got a bruise, he wouldn't even know how he got it.

"Imagine if he finds out about the 'Menshen stuff'!" Lu laughed to himself.

Menshen stuff, powers, mythical disease...my mind wandered off while walking to the city afar. I thought of the night when I saw Lingling after Pingye fell ill. The questions I hadn't thought about in a while reemerged.

Why did Lingling run in the rain with her pot? And it was right after Pingye fell into a coma! Did she really forget something that important or did she lie? It's possible that I was completely wrong, but two mysterious things happened back to back? The facts hit me right in the face.

How did Pingye fall into a coma? She showed no symptoms of any illness when I saw her the same day. Then again, I'm not a doctor or an expert in Chinese mythology. I don't know how likely a serious coma would develop so suddenly for a young person, unless Pingye already had an underlying disease. Normal medical knowledge wouldn't help here anyway. I shook away my thoughts.

The city came into view. Small and tall buildings were packed closely together. Right behind the city were gorgeous green mountains that were at least three times higher. A river ran down the middle, separating the city into two parts. Lu said it was Shiliuwan, a city outside of Hong Kong.

We found a dry market. In case you didn't know, a dry market is a grocery store where people sell processed or prepared foods. Chunks of ham were hung by the window to dry. We exchanged an excited look.

Inside, the market was crowded with people shoulder to shoulder. Aisles were so narrow that only two people could pass each other. Loud chatters were coming from all directions, almost sounding like people were arguing with one another. The checkout line was long.

Just when I was passing through the entrance, I bumped into a statue at the side of the door. It may be some sort of goat or an ox made of dark fur, definitely not stone or wood. The statue had a horn coming out of its forehead. *Why do so many mysterious animals have one horn?* Its deep eyes were staring right at me, which gave me goosebumps. The statue seemed alive except it hadn't flinched when I bumped into it. It was dead still.

We walked down the aisles in search of the packaged ham.

Whenever my eyes were within the range of that statue, I couldn't help looking at it. I felt an urge to check every few minutes. Do you ever have a feeling someone is watching you behind your back? That was how I felt in a crowded dry market.

We didn't need much else. Once I found boxes of ham, we snatched as many boxes as we could and headed for the cash register.

THE UNTOLD TRUTH OF CLUB 門神

"Are you kids alone?" The cashier asked once we got to the front of the line, eyeballing all the ham we put on the counter.

"No, our parents are waiting outside. They asked us to get some snacks...and ham," Lingling said calmly, handing over the money. We nodded.

"Alright, here's your change. Have a nice day."

You may wonder why I wrote about such a random conversation. Well, it was not random. The fact that one of us lied and the rest of us went along, even if it was for a plausible reason, is why the next fight took place.

I expected to feel a weight coming off my shoulders once we left the dry market, but I didn't. I kept telling myself it was a statue and there was no reason for me to worry.

I decided to look back one last time to get over it, but you may have guessed what happened. *The statue isn't there*, like in every horror movie. My breath became short, and my heart started racing. I hated to walk with the anxiety of the beast popping out in front of me at any second.

"Look." My voice was barely a whisper. No one heard. I took a deep breath and said again, "Everyone, look, the statue...." My voice trailed off, still shaking.

My friends turned their heads at once. There was shock in their eyes. Finally, someone spoke. "We need to go back to Shen, fast!"

I started to bolt back with everyone. I know I could never run that fast again. It was the fear that was fueling me. I ran for what felt like an eternity.

"Stop!" Lingling commanded. "I've been looking behind the entire time. *Nothing* is following us!"

It was only after I stopped running and realized that we weren't in any immediate danger, my legs started to ache severely.

"You know things like this can blend in," Lu said seriously.

"What if someone is in front of the statue blocking our view so we couldn't see it?" Bo came up with a scenario.

"Well, I'm not going back to check," Lu mumbled.

"No one is asking you to. I don't think we should panic if we don't need to," Lingling asserted.

"So, you really don't think anything is around." I still wasn't sure, glancing at all the possible places to hide.

"Nothing." Lingling's voice was reassuring.

We kept moving- walking this time. My steps were sluggish, being deprived of energy. The thing is, I believed Lingling when she said things like that, but I still sensed I was being watched. *At least it could be a false sense, right?*

Finally, I saw a familiar mountain in the distance just before I heard a loud gasp. Having a hunch of what it was, I wriggled. There were the creepy deep eyes and dark fur, except now the statue was standing nearby, ready to charge.

I instantly thought of the spear on my back. I had been mentally preparing for this moment ever since I bumped into the statue. Nevertheless, I stayed motionless, terrified how this beast would react if I moved. It stared at us from five meters away. The next thing I knew, everyone had a weapon in their hands within two seconds.

Using one word to sum up this fight-chaotic.

The beast charged and ran straight toward me! *Oh no.* Maybe it sensed I was the least prepared. *What am I supposed to do? Do I run? Or do I jab my spear at it, and hope for the best?* All the knowledge I had learned of what to do in a situation like this immediately disappeared.

Everyone saw what the beast was doing and stood beside me, which was brave but not wise. Think of it this way. If you don't want the arrow to hit the target, you don't make the target bigger and easier to hit!

I ran away toward the other side of the rocky beach, hoping my friends would fight the beast from a distance. However, the beast followed me closely and got within a few meters of me. At this moment, I knew I had no other options. I held my spear in my hand. With all my energy, I threw it, then turned around to run. I'm not an expert at this, but I'm pretty sure I wasn't supposed to run like that, or maybe I was.

Only I didn't run fast enough. With its head forward and horn pointing at me, the beast made a giant swing of its paw. It slashed my left arm before I slipped away. Assuming the beast was still after me, I kept running and the pain started to kick in. I tripped over a rock and glanced back.

My friends were caught in a furious fight. Mei stabbed the beast in its leg. It roared in outrage and swung its paw at Mei, who was quick to dodge it. The beast fell on its belly, while Mei held out her hand pointing at it. *Her spell?* The beast abruptly paused its motion for a split second, then resumed movement. Her power seemed to have worked on a monster, even though it was brief!

Bo struck the beast at its face with his spear, but the beast slapped it out of his hand. Without a weapon, Bo quickly drew out his silver plate, the gift from the moon goddess. He pointed it at the beast, changing angles and directions of the light beam.

The beast squinted at it. Furiously, it changed direction and charged toward Bo. This time, Bo put his hands up like a cross facing its horn. The silver plate dropped to the ground and rolled off. *He must be using his shield power.* Before I knew it, Bo was pushed down from the force of the beast's horn. He was almost run over but unharmed. The beast's clawed feet landed right next to him. If Bo had his arms out, he would have gotten stepped on. Bo bounced back up in the bat of an eye. The beast charged again, repeating the same motions. After the fourth time, Mei was finally able to pull Bo out of the pattern.

Lu stood aside, doing a straight point-and-shoot at the beast's chest. It landed on target, adding to the collection of arrows on its body. It must be hard to do because the beast kept moving and mixing with Menshens.

Lingling was on the shore with her arm outreached, three arrows floating in mid-air probably coated in water with additional arrows rising from the water.

The beast was charging and fighting. There were stab wounds and a handful of arrows all over its body.

My spear laid on the ground, not far from the fight. I started to stand up to grab it, even though my body screamed against it.

"Cassidy, stay over there!" Lingling locked eyes with me and yelled.

The beast turned to gaze at me, giving a shiver in my spine. All of a sudden, it leaped onto a hill and kept going until it was six meters up. No one could get to it as fast. The beast was facing me directly. My already racing heart was filled with terror.

THE UNTOLD TRUTH OF CLUB 門神

Suddenly, the beast jumped off the hill, straight at me. No no no! *I don't think I'll get out of this alive.* In my last-ditch effort to get up, I fell backward…again. The beast was crashing down, gaining speed every millisecond.

Out of nowhere, arrows flew through the air. Each one landed a direct hit on the beast's chest. The beast roared for the last time in mid-air and dropped to the ground like a rock. *THUMP*. Its body missed me by mere centimeters.

Still breathing heavily, I looked at the direction where the arrows came from. There was Lingling, standing tall with her arms still outstretched. I stared at her in awe, struggling to find my words. *I'm alive because of her.*

"It worked!" Lingling beamed.

"I've never seen you do that before!" Lu said in admiration.

"It's a new technique I've been practicing."

"Lingling is one of the best fighters in our school," Bo explained to me, dusting off his silver plate.

I was speechless. Even if I tried, I would choke on words from aftershock, pain and embarrassment. The cut was bothering me, but I didn't want to tell anyone. I dropped my head, either I was too ashamed or too weak to lift it. I hated being the one who had to be rescued all the time. *I can't fight. I'm not brave. I don't have any skills, and I don't know anything.*

"I think this beast may be a…" Bo was cut off by Lu.

"A Xiezhi (獬豸). See Bo, I know too! It's a beast that attacks anyone who lies in its presence. I bet it heard Lingling lying to the cashier and saw the rest of us nodded. That's why it attacked everyone."

Bo agreed with Lu. "Although," Bo said slowly with a grin, "I would've gone into details about how Xiezhi reinforced justice by killing guilty people. What you said is correct."

"That *is* what I said." Lu smirked, crossing his arms. "A truth monster."

"I wish we captured it alive," Lingling said wistfully. "Paiya Temple could keep a truth monster."

"For moving our coffins?" Mei said in an exaggerated voice. "There's not a chance in the universe we could restrain that thing on a leash."

"Even if we had a leash," Bo reasoned, "how do we get Xiezhi to Nasha Wetland, and bring it along while we look for the lotus flower? Not to mention convincing Shen to haul it."

"Speaking of the lotus flower," Lingling said, "we only have nine hours left. We need to get going *now*!"

We headed back to where Shen dropped us off. I looked to the left and right, front and back....*No! This is what I've been dreading.*

Shen was nowhere in sight.

CHAPTER 18:
THE MISSING DRAGON
February 7 (Wednesday 3:30 pm)

"**S**hen!" All of us called out in desperation. "Where are you?"

All I heard was the sound of the waves, mixed with a few seagulls squealing. No signs of Shen anywhere. Minutes passed, still not a trace.

"Something must...must have happened to Shen." Bo stumbled on his words. The fact was obvious.

The mood was gloomy, despite the sun shining brilliantly on us. Without Shen, we had absolutely no way of traveling. We lost our boats twice! There were less than nine hours left to use the scale, and we still needed to find the lotus flower seeds.

"Shen wouldn't leave us. It wants to eat the ham," I said. Stress gradually overtook my embarrassment from the last fight. I was determined to find Shen.

"Who knows?" Bo sighed. "Maybe it was sick of bringing us everywhere and abandoned us."

"It should be back soon, I hope," Mei said hesitantly.

"But how soon is *soon*? What if it turns out to be a day?" Bo said. "We don't have that kind of time!"

"So, what do you think we should do?!" Lu was losing patience, pacing back and forth.

"Why don't you try to think for once! I don't always have the answer!" Bo raised his voice.

"Well, you always act like you do!" Lu snapped back.

"Stop, stop!" I shouted, surprising myself. I wasn't the type of person to intervene like that, but I didn't want it to escalate. I paused, thinking about the rules of how to stop an argument smartly.

"Lu, we're all stressed," I finally said. "Bo, we're grateful you always provide us with information." I continued on, "All of us should make more of an effort to help, not always relying on you."

Moments of silence. I know we had a habit of relying on Bo in this sort of situation, without realizing it. Even myself, who knew him for only a few months.

"Sorry," Lu murmured.

"Sorry," Bo murmured back.

All of a sudden, I felt like a teacher. I didn't like it.

A Note to Self: How to Stop an Argument

You must appeal to both sides of the argument. Say why both are great. Make it sound like you fully understand why each person is acting that way, even if you don't. Don't openly take a side. Sometimes they're just in a bad mood and need to be calmed down, so use a soft voice. *Note: This advice is from a thirteen-year-old, not a professional, so take it at your own risk.*

Resume the story.

THE UNTOLD TRUTH OF CLUB 門神

Mei nudged my arm and said under her breath, "Since when did you become a mediator?"

I huffed a laugh. "Just now."

Looking out to the sea, the sun was still high. Bright orange buoys were bouncing with the endless blue waves in the distance. There was still not a single shadow of Shen.

"I mean we can make another raft, but that'll take too long." Bo got himself into a negative spiral. "Not to mention there are people around here. Someone is going to think we're running away from home. Then they'll call the authorities. We won't get back in time, and Pingye will die!" Bo was becoming louder by the second.

"Your yelling is going to make someone call the authorities." Lingling hushed Bo.

"Actually, we can't make another raft. We don't have any materials ready." Mei brought us back to reality. "We just have to find Shen."

"Well...." Lingling stood up. "I'm going to look for it. We can't waste any more time."

"Where?" Lu asked skeptically, "In the water? For how long? You'll pass out before you find it! You have to admit you have limits."

Lingling scowled. Apparently, she didn't like when Lu told her she couldn't do something. Nevertheless, she sighed. "At least, if I find Shen, I can ride it back."

"And if you don't find Shen?" Lu insisted.

Lingling shrugged. "If I get tired, I'll start swimming back. Okay?"

Suddenly, a light bulb flickered on in my head. "Ham!" I raised my voice in excitement. "We have ham!"

Everyone looked at me, baffled.

"Ham is the reason why Shen found us in the first place." I couldn't wait to blurt out my words. "It'll lead us to Shen!"

The idea dawned on everyone. We looked at each other and nodded with a knowing smirk. *We have our answer.*

"Well," Bo spoke in an intelligent voice, "our best chance of success is to divide and conquer."

"Right." We nodded.

Our plan was simple. We assigned an area for each of us (except Bo) to swim around carrying ham to lure Shen. As a safety measure, we agreed not to go beyond the twenty-five-meter radius offshore, and not to use the fire spell to conserve energy. This way, we would still be able to swim back if we were tired. Bo offered to do the fire spell for us when we take breaks. It sounded like a solid plan to me.

Four of us began to prepare for the plunge. We removed shoes, weapons, and emptied most of the supplies from our backpacks except ham. Bo lent me his bag. I peeked at my fresh wound from Xiezhi. It didn't seem too bad. I probably shouldn't go into the water, but I didn't want to miss out on the chance to save Shen and Pingye. *I'll just hide it. They won't let me go if they know.*

"Bo, don't lose the dragon scale." Lu delicately handed Bo a small box containing the precious ingredient for Pingye.

"Of course." Bo took it like a gem and mumbled to himself, "I'll have to learn how to swim. This is ridiculous. Well, I did try to learn many times...."

We got to the water in no time. The cold sea water was rising up my ankles with each wave. It wasn't long before the water reached my arms and chest. The second my wound touched the water, it was on fire. I winced. Eventually, my feet kicked into the bottomless ocean.

Swimming, huffing, and puffing. The pain subsided after I got used to it. Obviously, a lot more energy was needed to swim against the high tide. Lingling was way ahead of us. Propelled by her water power, she was gliding and faster than anyone else. Lu was the second behind Lingling, doing this old-fashioned thing called swimming.

"Don't wear yourself out, Lingling!" I yelled at her even though she may not hear me. "It's high tide!"

Soon four of us separated in four directions, covering each territory. From left to right, it was Lingling, myself, Mei and Lu.

CRASH, my head became submerged under a surface wave, one of many. My hair draped all over my face in a complete tangled mess that would take days to unknot. Fighting against the strong undercurrents, my energy was running lower and lower. I started shivering even though the sun was beaming down.

Minutes later, my muscles were about to give up. I decided to swim back for a break. It was comforting to see Bo standing on the shore waiting for me. Barely catching my breath, I got up from the water, cold and exhausted. Bo came up to me with a concerned look, holding a water bottle in one hand.

"Don't move, Cassidy." He started the fire spell. Immediately, the feeling of warm pricks and needles ran through my body. *This is exactly what I needed.*

Bo made sure I had recovered before letting me go back to the water again. Mei and Lu took breaks as well, but

Lingling had been out in the water the entire time. At one of my breaks, I asked Bo about it.

"Don't worry. Lingling has water power," Bo told me confidently.

"She still has limits, right?"

"Yes, but she knows her capability better than anyone else."

I was still worried, so I told myself to watch out for Lingling as her territory was next to mine.

After having to take multiple breaks, I was doubtful how long I could keep up with this. *Come on, Shen. Where are you?* Swimming and looking around, I suddenly realized Lingling was going further out into the ocean, which was well beyond the twenty-five-meter radius we agreed upon.

"Lingling, turn around!" I yelled, not sure if she could hear me. *Wait, is she swimming toward the orange buoys? Why?*

I swam closer to get her attention. "Lingling!" Salt water filled my mouth as I screamed, tasting like poison.

Finally, Lingling turned her head and began treading water, waiting for me to catch up.

"You can't be going this far. You haven't taken a break," I said while spitting salty water out of my mouth.

"Hold on." Lingling signaled behind her. "Look!"

I stared at the buoys. They were shaking violently, practically jumping in and out of the water. It couldn't possibly be caused by the waves.

"What do you think?" I asked with hope. *Could it be Shen underneath?*

THE UNTOLD TRUTH OF CLUB 門神

"I don't know, but I'll go look. You never know." Lingling took a deep breath, ready to plunge under the water.

The idea of her diving alone concerned me, as Lingling had been swimming nonstop the entire time. I was fearful this may be beyond her limits.

"I'm going with you."

"No," Lingling blurted in an instant.

"I *promise* I'll stay close." I was sure of it. I knew she'd do the same for me.

Lingling paused for a moment and said, "Fine, I might need some help, but make sure to follow my directions."

She took another deep breath, so did I. Facing each other, I held up my hand to signify the countdown. Three fingers; Two fingers; and one.

We dove. Instantly, the warm sun rays were gone. The only things visible were the murky green water and the occasional floating seaweed, accompanied by the muffled sound of waves.

Soon, a dark thread of rope came into view from the blurry void. Then another rope, and one more. They were vibrating like a mini earthquake underneath it. The ropes criss-crossed each other, shaping like small rectangles and parallelograms of some sort. They stretched out and eventually connected to the orange buoys above them.

Finally, I made out what it was, *a fishing net*. My heart was pumping with anticipation. I swam alongside the net, with Lingling closeby. The wobbling became more and more violent. Another stroke and I saw…scales, hundreds of scales. In the haze of it all was Shen, our sea dragon friend.

Shen was tangled, fighting furiously to escape the fishing net. Its head was caught in a rip of the net. The harder Shen wiggled, the tighter the rope became around its neck. Each scale acted like a hook preventing Shen from slipping out.

Shen stopped moving for a moment, as if it was expecting us. It must have smelled the ham. *Our plan worked.* Shen stared at me with pleading eyes, making a deep groaning sound.

Shen was suffocating, so was I. My chest was squeezing as I needed to breath air badly. I signaled for it to wait before having to kick back to the surface. Lingling was already floating above me.

My head broke the surface. I took in a big mouthful of air. Nearby, Lingling's limp body was thrown by the waves. Her usual bun was completely loose, and her long hair was drifting with the tide. She started to sink.

"Lingling!" I grabbed her desperately and held her horizontally while treading water. Her body was loose, her eyes closed and her face as pale as white paper. I was terrified. Looking around for help, I saw Mei swimming towards us.

"Mei!" I screamed.

"What happened?" Mei got to us as fast as she could. "I was coming to check on you."

"Lingling passed out!"

Mei quickly assessed her. "She's still breathing," Mei assured me, which made me feel a bit relieved. "She must have overused her power. We have to go back now!" Mei said in an urgent tone.

THE UNTOLD TRUTH OF CLUB 門神

"Wait. We found Shen!" I blurted out. "Its neck is restrained by the fishing net. I don't know how long it'll last!" I pointed at the quivering buoys near me.

Mei's eyes became wider, with a look of disbelief hogging her face. She stared at me and said, "Wait here. I'll release Shen."

Mei took out her knife from her backpack and disappeared into the water. As much as I wanted to follow her and help, I had to stay with Lingling. Even if I were to cut the net, I didn't know if there was a knife in the backpack that Bo gave me.

Anxiously watching the orange buoys jumping, I waited while holding Lingling in the water. I grew inpatient. My legs were getting sorer by the second. In the distance, Lu was racing over but it would take more than a minute for him to get here.

Lingling and Shen could die and I'm doing nothing about it. That fact exerted itself in my psyche, then stamped itself and mailed it to my brain. I felt powerless.

The sun started to set. The air felt colder and the wind whistled in my ears. I stared at the buoys like a hawk gawking its prey. My leg muscles were burning from treading water for too long. I started to worry about Mei as well. *Did she find Shen? Did she get stuck too?*

A big wave came straight at my head. I quickly lifted Lingling's head higher. Once the wave passed, I noticed the buoys had stopped bouncing around. *What's happening?* I was on edge.

CRASH, the water exploded in front of my eyes, sending a wall of waves to the air. The water fell back down, revealing hundreds of scales. There, Shen shone brilliantly in the sunset, with its head pointing to the sky majestically for a few seconds. Then it flapped around in the water, making big splashes. I let out a long sigh, never so happy to see a sea dragon frolicking.

Mei popped up next to it, taking in huge gulps of breath. "Mei! You did it!"

"Hand me Lingling," Mei pulled herself onto Shen. "We don't have much time left to use the scale."

I swam over. Mei secured Lingling in her lap and offered me a hand. Just when I was getting on Shen, my left foot was suddenly caught by something. I was being dragged down!

I twitched. The memories of fear and hopelessness from the White Cloth Demon flooded me instantly. I looked down at my foot in despair, expecting nothing less than a White Cloth.

Oh. It's the fishing net. I was relieved when the old, worn, and intertwined ropes emerged from under the water, still attached to my left foot. Holding on Mei, I unraveled the ropes with my other hand and swung myself on the back of Shen.

Lu finally got to us. "Is Lingling okay?" He asked anxiously while catching his breath.

"She passed out!" Mei and I answered simultaneously.

"What?" Lu hopped on Shen immediately. "Shen, get back to shore!"

Shen swam back and let us off. Joined by Bo, we laid Lingling on the ground and sat around her.

Mei told me a while ago that it's dangerous for Menshens to overuse powers because they would pass out. Most of the time they'll wake up, but they may end up being

THE UNTOLD TRUTH OF CLUB 門神

incredibly sick. In fact, not overusing powers was one of the most important things taught to us.

Why did Lingling do it when she knew this would happen?

"Lingling!" Lu yelled and shook her shoulders.

"Shh...." Mei stopped Lu from shaking. She held Lingling's head on her lap, carefully watching her breathing, feeling her forehead, and checking her pulse. "She's fine for the most part, although I don't know for sure," Mei said.

"You're right." Lu let go of Lingling's shoulders. "Lingling will probably wake up soon."

With things seemingly calming down and my adrenaline rush fading away, the throbbing pain on my arm intensified. I grimaced, even the smallest touch made my arm burn. I looked down. It was no longer a small superficial cut. Now my forearm was red and swelling around the cut.

"Cassidy, your arm..." Bo said in horror.

"You didn't tell us you were wounded!" Lu said loudly.

"Oh, my goodness," Mei sighed. She walked over to the pile of supplies dumped from our backpacks and picked out a first-aid kit. She cleaned and applied antibacterial cream to my wound, while I winced from the momentary pain. "Why?" Mei asked seriously.

"Why what?"

"Why didn't you say anything? Look! You're getting an infection!" Mei began wrapping gauze around my arm.

"I didn't know it would get this bad. It was a small cut," I murmured. *What can I say-If I told you, you wouldn't let me search in the water?*

"This is a wound from Xiezhi, right? A monster with who-knows-what on its claw scraped your arm." Mei finished with wrapping. "Make sure to let me know whenever you get cut or hurt by something, so I can clean and bandage it. Your wound could've gotten really bad if not treated by antibiotics."

I nodded. With gauze covering most of my forearm, I felt better somehow.

"Does it feel alright?" Mei asked.

I nodded.

"Are you sure?"

I nodded again.

"Completely sure?"

I nodded again, again.

"Meat." A deep raspy voice came from behind me. "Meat Holder?"

I turned around, feeling embarrassed about forgetting the ham. We rummaged through all the backpacks, dug out ham and tossed it to Shen. One after the other, Shen shoved it down its throat in an instant. After all the ham was gone, Shen belched loudly. Then it did this weird thing with its mouth, which resembled a smile.

"We need to go now." I smiled back at Shen.

Riding on a content Shen, we headed to Nasha wetland without further delay. At this point, we had seven hours left.

CHAPTER 17:
THE WEATHERED NOTEBOOK

February 7 (Wednesday 5:30 pm)

Searching for a flower and collecting its seeds. It sounds easy, right? Compared to cutting off a scale from a live dragon, finding a flower sounded calm and stress-free. But it wasn't.

Lingling finally woke up during the ride. "Shen!" That was the first word she blurted out.

"You're awake!" We shouted with glee.

"What happened?" Lingling blinked, sitting up from Mei's lap. She looked around, taking in the surroundings.

"You passed out, but we found Shen!" Lu said.

Shen groaned in response.

"Are you feeling okay?" I asked.

"I think so, just a little drowsy...." Lingling let out a coughing fit.

"Lingling, I don't think you should come with us to search for the lotus flower," Mei voiced firmly. "You should stay behind with Shen."

"No, no, no, I want to help."

"This is exactly what made you pass out, not accepting rest." Lu leaned to the side to see Lingling.

"Look, I don't even have to do anything. I'll stay right next to you. Whenever there's a danger, I'll stay out of it."

"We don't want you to pass out again," I pleaded.

"It feels like getting over a cold. Besides, one extra pair of eyes won't hurt."

Mei bit her lip and said at last, "Fine, but only if you stay right next to me."

"And do *not* fight under any circumstances," Lu added.

Lingling sighed in relief. "Sure. Thank you."

After we got off Shen, we swam as close as possible to Nasha Wetland without being seen. This place was beautiful. Narrow strips of the grassland divided the water into squares. After passing through a wall of trees, we saw hundreds of lily pads and colorful flowers, partially hidden from view.

We took the narrow wooden bridge over the water, occasionally passing random people. I glanced at each flower, which all looked the same to me. What we needed was a flower that stood out from the rest, *hopefully*.

"Let's go to the shadier parts. I don't think a magic flower would be out in the open," Mei stated rationally, walking next to Lingling.

"What about over there?" I pointed to a densely overgrown area. We agreed and started searching everywhere, every nook and cranny, and under the leaves of plants.

Then I felt...something on my ankle.

"Cassidy, don't move," Mei said seriously.

I froze. I slowly looked down. A snake was slowly making its way up my leg. *I hate snakes.* Although compared to the other situations I've been in on this trip, this was a walk in the park. According to Mei, I would be fine as long as I stayed still. *She knows snakes.* It wasn't that dangerous of a situation except...you know, icky.

I listened to Mei's advice and tried my best to stay still while the snake slowly crawled its way up. It was freaky. By the time it slithered its way up to my hand with a cold scaly touch, I immediately jerked it off without thinking, and without realizing the consequences.

Suddenly, hissing erupted from all around me. Numerous snakes emerged from nowhere and threw themselves at us! They were climbing up my legs and wrapping around my body. Did I already tell you I hate snakes? The same thing happened to everyone else. Before we knew it, ten or twenty snakes were on each of us. We were screaming and grabbing the snakes at the same time. It was complete chaos.

I was mortified when one of the snakes started to squeeze my chest, making it hard for me to breathe. My intuition was to yank it off my chest at once, but the harder I tugged, the tighter it got.

"I can't breathe!" I screamed using all my remaining energy, while taking short shallow breaths.

"Grab seven inches below its head! That's where the heart is!" Mei yelled.

It was either that or let the snake kill me. I closed my eyes and turned my face away while I squeezed the snake's neck as hard as I could. *Ugh!*

Then everything suddenly stopped. All the snakes were turned mute. Out of the bushes appeared a snake with silver skin hissing in high pitch. It stood out from the rest, looking pristine and elegant. With each hiss it made, more and more snakes retreated.

Once all of them retreated into the forest, the snake with silver skin was the last one remaining. It picked its head up elegantly, swung from left to right with its imaginary hair, then slithered away from us. After moving two meters in that direction, it turned its head to look at us again. It jerked its head forward, moved, jerked again, then moved forward.

"I think it wants us to follow," Mei stated, still surprised.

"I don't think we should. Why do other snakes listen to it? Maybe it's feared by others." Lingling yawned.

"Are you sure?" I speculated. "I think we should follow the snake. It seemed to have helped us with, you know-not dying?"

"Don't forget we killed some snakes, so it could be plotting a revenge," Lingling said in defense.

"I agree with Cassidy." Bo spoke in an intelligent tone. "Besides, it's unlikely a snake could make that complicated plan to lure prey by trust."

"Well, let's vote." Mei stepped in. "Who doesn't want to follow the snake?"

"Lu?" Lingling said as she put up her hand.

"Sorry. I'm going to vote for the snake side." Awkward silence. I could feel the repeated tension between the twins on this trip.

The snake side won, with four to one votes.

I walked along with Mei. "How did you know to grab seven inches below the snake's neck, Mei? You saved my life!" I think it's a little ironic that Mei wants to help the earth, save animals and all, but she knows exactly how to kill one. Knowledge comes handy, right?

"Well, when you research plants and animals, you learn a few things." Mei quickly changed to a serious tone. "Please, Cassidy. Next time stay still. If you had stayed still, none of the snakes would be killed."

I felt awful about myself. It was me, again. "Sorry, I promise I won't do it again." I really meant it.

"Alright, I understand." Mei comforted me.

It didn't make me feel much better. The last situation could've ended much worse if the silver-skin snake didn't help. *Mei knows what to do with animals. She probably already encountered this before, so I just have to listen.*

The snake led us onto the wooden walkways over the water and through a line of trees. In front of us was a large triangular lake. The snake continued along the lake then made a sharp turn. It slithered through bushes, then through a thick set of trees. We followed closely with the tall grass brushing against our legs. After passing through the trees, what I expected to see was another open field of some sort, but that was not what I saw.

Imagine walking into a house and expecting to see an average interior, but instead, it's a palace inside! The air instantly became warm and humid, which felt like a rain forest. The trees were twice in height but thin as a twig. A straight trail was in the middle.

It felt different. The air, the light, the scent, the sight, and practically everything! If I didn't know, I would have never guessed I was only a few trees away from Nasha wetland. *What is this place?*

The snake continued to lead us on long winding trails, with such certainty that it must've known this place like the back of its hand, except it didn't have hands. The trail twisted and turned without showing anything new, not something that would indicate the existence of a magic flower. For all I knew, it could have been leading us in loops for hours.

We turned another corner, and...*a dead end?* There was a barrier of trees blocking where the trail would have continued. I couldn't believe the two-and-a-half-hour long hike led us to this! We looked at each other in silence. We must have gone the wrong way. However, the snake kept on going and slithered through the barrier.

What do we do now?

"Hey! SNAKE! Where are you going?" Lingling yelled, scaring off birds.

"I don't think it's coming back," Mei said in a sore tone.

"It has too. It can't leave us here. We've been following for hours!" Lu refused to give up.

"It doesn't even know where we need to go," Bo said slowly.

The truth dawned on me. "Right. We followed a random snake hoping it'll lead us to the right place, but it wouldn't know."

"I think we should go back to where we started." Lingling sounded pessimistic.

It was a depressing thought. More or less, we were in the wrong direction.

"No! We are not leaving." Lu exclaimed, as if it was the most obvious thing in the world, "The snake wouldn't lead us to nowhere. Maybe…it can read minds?"

"What?" That sounded ludicrous to me.

"I don't know…." Lu doubted himself as well.

"Yeah-no, a snake can't do that," I said. Thinking back on it, I don't think I should have made that statement. I didn't know anything about magic reptiles, or what they are capable of doing.

"My point is, the snake wouldn't lead us here for no reason," Lu repeated.

"Lead us where, Lu?" Lingling shot back. "I don't know if you noticed, but we're at a dead end."

Lu scratched his head. "Maybe we should follow it through the trees?"

"I mean…we could try." Bo pondered. "The barrier may be thin like a maze, or it may lead to something else."

"I say we cut a few trees down." Lingling shrugged.

"Wait! We don't know how many trees are behind, or maybe some monster is waiting to attack us!" Mei countered.

"No monster is hiding in the shadows waiting to eat our brains, Mei." Lu was losing his patience.

"You don't know that."

"But the important thing is we have only four hours and twenty minutes left to use the scale." I looked at Lingling's watch. I had been counting down the hours and minutes.

Mei paused and took a deep breath, like a teacher about to give a long lecture. "If you have to cut the trees down, do it for Pingye's sake. But I won't let you do it under any other circumstances. Make sure to cut as few as possible."

"Thank you!" Bo and I walked over to give Mei a quick hug. Lingling and Lu took out knives from their backpack and began cutting.

"Did you really think I would choose trees over Pingye?" Mei murmured.

I only knew Mei for a few months, but it felt like I've known her for so much longer. Allowing us to cut down trees was huge for Mei. *She's probably going to have us replant every tree we take down.*

The trees were unlike those in the actual Nasha wetlands. In the magical part, they were tall twigs with some leaves all packed together like small crayons in an even smaller box. Bo and I began to cut trees as well, only I had to take a lot of breaks because the wound on my arm still hurt.

CRACK, the last tree we needed to cut fell down. I squeezed through a narrow path, and spotted an oval pond surrounded by twig-like trees. Under the moonlight, the pond was shimmering with the moon's reflection in the water surrounded by countless white flowers. Not even one shred of wind. It was surreal.

In the center was a white lotus flower that stood out from the rest, with its petals glowing elegantly, and the brightness making the surrounding water look like glittering silver. In front of us was the silver snake, the knowing all and "mind-reading" snake, sprawled on the ground waiting patiently.

THE UNTOLD TRUTH OF CLUB 門神

We cheered in excitement. After going through many life-threatening experiences on this trip, finding the flower was a big relief.

Without hesitation, Lu jumped into the water. As soon as he made a splash, hundreds and thousands of bees erupted from nowhere, like opening up Pandora's Box! The loud buzzing noises and moving shadows instantly surrounded us. Lu quickly got out of the water and fell backward. The bees flew in a loose circle over us, as if debating whether we were worth stinging. I was petrified.

In a nick of time, the silver-skin snake bared its fangs and made high pitched hisses. More and more bees flew away from us with each hiss. The sound of buzzing was becoming faint. All bees were now hovering directly above the lotus flower. Not attacking us, but not leaving either.

"I think the bees are protecting the lotus flower," Lu whispered. "They're going to attack anyone who touches it."

Lingling glanced at the swarm. "Yeah. They're guarding it with their lives."

"We need to think of a different way to get to the flower." Mei was certain of it.

Bo nodded. "I agree. They'll sting us without mercy."

Everyone else was bouncing around ideas. Lu suggested wrapping himself up completely in extra clothes and going for it, but we weren't sure if it would be enough. Mei said she knew of some natural herbs that can heal bee stings, but she didn't know if she could find them here.

I was perplexed. The snake saved us twice already. Obviously, it could be trusted. Then why did it lead us into the apparently "unsafe" situation? I believe this snake was able to control the bees, like what it did with the rest of the snakes. Maybe the bees simply stayed there to make sure we don't damage the flower.

"Cassidy?" Lingling interrupted my train of thoughts. "You didn't say anything. What are you thinking?"

"Maybe...we should trust the snake," I said carefully. "Now that it's here, I don't think the bees will attack us." I was waiting for them to burst out with logical reasons why I was wrong. Even worse, they were silent.

After I explained it one more time, Bo countered, "The bees surrounded Lu and were about to sting him."

"But that was *before* the snake hissed at the bees to stay away!" I emphasized.

"It's still too risky to send anyone over," the rest of them agreed with Bo.

"We don't have any other ways." I defended my theory. "More importantly, we don't have time to figure it out!"

Just when I spoke those words, Ms. Wu's voice came to my head. "*Always listen to Menshens.*" I hesitated. I took another glance at the snake. It was looking at me calmly, as if to reassure me. Somehow, I felt convinced. *I can trust it.* It wouldn't lead us here to be harmed.

"I'll go." The words coming from my mouth surprised me. "I'll get the seeds. I'm sure bees won't sting me." *Am I being dumb?*

"No, Cassidy. I won't let you go." Mei sighed. "I'll go, I guess."

"No," I said firmly, "I don't want you to risk your life with my idea."

"You haven't done anything like this before." Mei was deeply worried.

"It doesn't make a difference. You can't tell me you have experience picking Lotus flower seeds under a bunch of flying bees."

"Your wound is infected," Mei insisted.

"But I felt better already." I turned to the glimmering water and took off my shoes.

"Wait! Wait! Wait!" An outburst of shouts came from each direction.

"No, Cassidy!"

"I'll go!"

I was determined not to let anyone else take the risk. It was my idea after all. I stepped into the water, and my feet glazed over the soft round pebbles step by step.

The buzzing sound grew louder when I got closer. I pressed my hands to my ears as the noise was deafening. Slowly the water became deeper. I started to swim toward the circle of bees. My heart was beating faster with each stroke. At this moment, I could only see three things, water, the lotus flower, and a dark cloud of thousands and thousands of bees above my head.

This is probably a bad idea. But I can't back out now. I'm not a coward.

A warm golden glow illuminated from the lotus flower surrounded me. A comforting glow. The magical flower was right in front of me, with its seeds located in the center shaped like an upside-down green cone. With a trembling hand, I reached for the flower. The bees were screaming in my ear so much that it almost broke my eardrums. I took a deep breath and in one movement, I plucked a seed.

I shut my eyes tight, waiting for the painful stings. One, two, five seconds went by. *Nothing.* I was so relieved I could cry! I opened my eyes and kept gathering the seeds one by one. *Six*, I counted in my palm. I clenched them in a tight fist to make sure they wouldn't fall through.

I swam back as fast as I could, with the water splashing behind me. Once I got out of the water, I was immediately wrapped in hugs and praises.

"Cassidy! You did it!" My friends raved about how "brave" and "daring" I was.

I was nearly squished to death by them. I couldn't make out any words. I grinned, proud that I was finally able to do something unimaginable.

"Can I look at the seeds?" Lu asked.

They backed off slightly to let me open my palms. Everyone circled around to admire the six white seeds, still wet and shining under the moonlight. Since I no longer had my backpack, Lingling carefully took them from my palms and put them in a small box.

By this time, all the bees disappeared. It felt surreal. *The trip is over, the dangers are gone, the mysteries are solved...wait, no. They aren't, not yet at least. There are still so many unanswered questions.*

"What's the fastest way to get out?" asked Mei, looking around.

"Well, the safest way is to go back where we came," Bo perked up and signaled the snake. Slowly hissing, the silver-skin snake led us back through the winding paths. We were able to follow the snake easily with its silver skin reflecting the moonlight like a natural flashlight.

Finally, we were back to the usual, or unusual Nasha Wetland.

THE UNTOLD TRUTH OF CLUB 門神

It was time to part with the silver snake. I waved goodbye, being grateful for all the help we received but also feeling like losing a close friend. I'd probably never see it again. Just when I was about to leave, I heard a soft hissing voice.

"I am Wei...sssss...." Wei quickly disappeared into the bushes.

"WAIT! You talk?" Lu yelled.

Wei was already gone. No sight of it anymore.

I don't even know how to comment on a talking snake. *It's weird* - would be the thing to say, but I felt like I said it a lot. It's the new normal. My life is now revolving around weirdness.

Both the dragon scale and lotus flower seeds were collected. All we needed to do was head straight back to school, but something else happened.

Moments before we got on Shen, a ginormous bird surrounded by a glow of light flew directly over my head out of nowhere. The bird had to be two meters tall!

"我的天啊!" I yelled (meaning my sky). Everyone ducked as it made a loud whooshing noise close to our heads.

The bird landed gracefully in front of me, with its soft golden glare beaming onto us. The bird's tail was radiant red, white, blue, black, and yellow. It was beautiful, elegant, and a little odd looking containing body parts of various animals. I thought I may have seen this kind of bird in Chinese traditional paintings. Based on its look, I could tell it was not an ordinary bird.

An object the bird was holding with its claw caught my attention. It looked like a notebook. Gray, dirty, and old looking, like it was one hundred years old laying on the ground eroding the entire time. The bird flew a little bit to get off the ground then dropped the old notebook right in front of me. The bird bowed to me before it took off.

I stared quietly at the bird flying away.

"A Fenghuang." Bo was awestruck. "I never thought I would get to see one of those in real life."

Fenghuang. I'm not sure why it gave me a notebook, but that question can wait.

Once Fenghuang disappeared into the darkness, I pointed my flashlight at the notebook, examining it in disbelief.

Mei broke the silence. "Well, look inside."

I got on my knees, picked it up, and started to flip through the tattered yellow pages. It had random numbers, with no clear connections, and a sketch of something shaped like a water drop, with a very faint blue green-ish color. More sketches, more numbers, crossed-out numbers, and really big numbers. I imagine all the information would take years to write down.

Why did Fenghuang deliver it to me?

"What are you going to do with it?" asked Lingling.

For once, I wasn't the one asking the question. I was answering it, but without an answer.

"I don't know, but it's probably important."

CHAPTER 18:
MYSTERIES DEEPEN
February 8 (Thursday 12:00 am)

It took us half an hour to get back to school, with only fifteen minutes to spare before the scale lost its power. It was late at night. Dark, quiet, and eerie, the three things you never want a place to be simultaneously.

We ran to the clinic, our footsteps cutting into the silence. Someone poked her head out behind the clinic door down the hallway. It was Ms. Wu.

"Hurry! These are the last two ingredients we need!" hastily said Ms. Wu.

Lu and Lingling rushed to the door and handed over the dragon scale and lotus seeds in a rush.

"The dragon scale has to be used in ten minutes, or else it won't work!" Lu yelled, wiping off sweat from his face.

Pingye's bed was behind a curtain. A nurse swiftly put the seeds and scale under a grinder and started to swirl and press intensely at the same time. Minutes later, she collected all the dust and placed it in a small tube full of clear liquid. The tube was put on a vortex shaking violently before all contents completely dissolved. Without a second delay, the nurse pulled a long syringe to suck up all the precious medicine and walked over to Pingye's bed.

I took a deep breath after the nurse came out from behind the curtain with an empty syringe. She gave us a reassuring nod. *Pingye is going to be safe. All our hard work paid off.*

"Great job! I'm glad you're all safe," Ms. Wu said in a soft voice. She patted my back with a smile. "I'm so proud of all of you. Now please go back to your rooms. Pingye needs time to recover."

Someone shut the door. Silence crept in again. *So, is that it?*

Thinking there was nothing else I could do to help at the moment, I came back to my room and cleaned up. Mei put fresh gauze on my arm before I got into bed. It still stung but I was used to it at this point. Mei and I talked about making chicken soup for Pingye tomorrow, or something to celebrate her recovery.

I needed to relax after such a journey, but my brain was still in overdrive. I couldn't see myself falling asleep anytime soon, so I got up and poured myself a cup of hot green tea. I started writing in my diary about things that had been on my mind lately.

I need to keep track of all the mysteries. There are so many! What really happened to Pingye that night? How did the snake Wei know what we wanted? Does the riddle lead to the missing books? What was the flying golden ring? What happened to Zheng? Why did Lingling say her dad died when she was little, but Lu said he came back when they were seven? How did Principal Song disappear? Is it normal to have so many mysteries in a Menshen school?

Yet, the important question that's always on my mind is-why am I here? Why was I sent to this school even though I'm not a Menshen? Principal Jiang never answered my "good" question.

Most recently, my newly collected notebook, given to me by Fenghuang. *Why is the notebook given to me?* I'm starting to think maybe I am supposed to be here for some bizarre reason. I should take a closer look at the notebook and maybe….

Wait! I heard a scream. Should I check it out? It's the middle of the night, but I think I need to.

Maybe it's about Pingye.

Main Characters
Cassidy Giordano 卡西迪
Bo Chen 陈波
Lingling Sun 孙玲玲
Lu Sun 孙露
Mei Cao 曹梅

Side Characters
Guo Qin 秦果
Hao 好
Ke Zhang 张克
Li'an Yang 杨丽安
Ming He 何明
Monk Taiyuan 太元和尚
Mr. Peng 彭先生
Mr. Wang 王先生
Ms. Fan 范女士
Ms. Wu 吴女士
Pingye Yu 余萍叶
Principal Jiang 江校长
Principal Song 宋校长
Yao Yao 姚瑶
Yi Han 韩艺

Gods
Chang'e 嫦娥 Goddess of the moon
Chenghuang 城隍神 God of walls and moats
Gonggong 龚工 God of water
Goumang 句芒 God of wood and spring

Hebo 河伯 God of the Yellow River
Jade Emperor 玉皇 God of all heavens
Lu Ban 鲁班 God of craftsmanship
Meng Po 孟婆 Goddess of forgetfulness
Nuwa 女娲 Creator of humans
Queen Mother of the West 西王母
Shujun 叔均 God of agriculture
Shunfeng'er 顺风耳 God of hearing
Tianhou (Mazu) 天后 (媽祖) Goddess of the sea
Zhurong 祝融 God of fire

Mythical Creatures
Bixi 赑屃
Fenghuang 凤凰
Qingniao 青鸟
Shen 蜃
Wei 瑋
White cloth demon 白布怪
Xiezhi 獬豸
Zheng 狰

ACKNOWLEDGEMENTS

I wouldn't be able to do an acknowledgments page in this book without mentioning my mother, Tracy Chen, for the countless hours she spent reading, editing, and helping me with this book. Many times, I would call it 'our book' without correcting myself because while she didn't write the book, she helped make this book into what it is today.

I was inspired to write a story surrounding mythology of my own, after reading the series of The Heroes of Olympus by Rick Riordan. Thank you for the inspiration.

To the people who read this book in its earliest version, thank you for the priceless feedback.

To my teachers who encouraged me to write this book, and answered my questions when I needed them, you're amazing.

Lastly, I hope you enjoyed this adventure with Cassidy, and look forward to more. Thank you from the bottom of my heart for taking time to read this book,

ABOUT THE AUTHOR

Hemie Yao published her debut novel, The Untold Truth of Club 門神: The Mission, at the age of twelve. Daughter of a Chinese immigrant, she lives in New Hampshire and grows up in a mixed culture background. She loves to immerse herself in nature, art, and fictional worlds.

Credits Will be Given in The Final Book

Also note that most of this book is based on facts I believe to be true of Chinese mythology, but a few aren't.

Made in the USA
Middletown, DE
06 December 2023